P9-DFI-430

Prostate Cancer

Titles in the Diseases and Disorders series include:

DISEASES &
DISORDERS

Prostate Cancer

Barbara Sheen

LUCENT BOOKS
A part of Gale, Cengage Learning

GALE
CENGAGE Learning

Detroit • New York • San Francisco • New Haven, Conn • Waterville, Maine • London

Property of Library
Cape Fear Community College

GALE
CENGAGE Learning™

© 2008 Gale, Cengage Learning

ALL RIGHTS RESERVED. No part of this work covered by the copyright herein may be reproduced, transmitted, stored, or used in any form or by any means graphic, electronic, or mechanical, including but not limited to photocopying, recording, scanning, digitizing, taping, Web distribution, information networks, or information storage and retrieval systems, except as permitted under Section 107 or 108 of the 1976 United States Copyright Act, without the prior written permission of the publisher.

Every effort has been made to trace the owners of copyrighted material.

LIBRARY OF CONGRESS CATALOGING-IN-PUBLICATION DATA
Sheen, Barbara. Prostate cancer / by Barbara Sheen. p. cm. -- (Diseases and disorders) Includes bibliographical references and index. ISBN 978-1-59018-593-3 (hardcover) 1. Prostate--Cancer--Juvenile literature. I. Title. RC280.P7S54 2008 616.99'463--dc22
2008003808

Lucent Books
27500 Drake Rd
Farmington Hills MI 48331

ISBN-13: 978-1-59018-593-3
ISBN-10: 1-59018-593-5

Printed in the United States of America
2 3 4 5 6 7 12 11 10 9 8

Table of Contents

"The Most Difficult Puzzles Ever Devised"

Charles Best, one of the pioneers in the search for a cure for diabetes, once explained what intrigued him so about medical research: "It's not just the gratification of knowing one is helping people," he confided, "although that probably is a more heroic and selfless motivation. Those feelings may enter in, but truly, what I find best is the feeling of going toe to toe with nature, of trying to solve the most difficult puzzles ever devised. The answers are there somewhere, those keys that will solve the puzzle and make the patient well. But how will those keys be found?"

Since the dawn of civilization, nothing has so puzzled people—and often frightened them, as well—as the onset of illness in a body or mind that seemed healthy before. Being unable to reverse conditions such as a seizure, the inability of a heart to pump, or the sudden deterioration of muscle tone in a small child, or even to understand why they occur was unspeakably frustrating to healers. Even before there were names for such conditions, before they were understood at all, each was a reminder of how complex the human body was and how vulnerable.

While our grappling with understanding diseases has been frustrating at times, it has also provided some of humankind's most heroic accomplishments. Alexander Fleming's accidental discovery in 1928 of a mold that could be turned into penicillin has resulted in the saving of untold millions of lives. The isolation of the enzyme insulin has reversed what was once a death sentence for anyone with diabetes. There also have been great strides in combating conditions for which there is not yet a cure. Medicines can help AIDS patients live longer, diagnostic tools such as mammography and ultrasounds can help doctors find tumors while they are treatable, and laser surgery techniques have made the most intricate, minute operations routine.

This "toe-to-toe" competition with diseases and disorders is even more remarkable when viewed in a historical continuum. An astonishing amount of progress has been made in a very short time. Just two hundred years ago, the existence of germs as a cause of some diseases was unknown. In fact, less than 150 years ago a British surgeon named Joseph Lister had difficulty persuading his fellow doctors that washing their hands before delivering a baby might increase the chances of a healthy delivery (especially if they had just attended to a diseased patient)!

Each book in Lucent's Diseases and Disorders series explores a disease or disorder and the knowledge that has been accumulated (or discarded) by doctors through the years. Each book also examines the tools used for pinpointing a diagnosis, as well as the various means that are used to treat or cure a disease. Finally, new ideas are presented—techniques or medicines that may be on the horizon.

Frustration and disappointment are still part of medicine because not every disease or condition can be cured or prevented. But the limitations of knowledge are constantly being pushed outward; the "most difficult puzzles ever devised" are finding challengers every day.

Lifesaving Information

In 1999, as a result of a routine physical exam, Joe Torre, former manager of the New York Yankees baseball team, was diagnosed with prostate cancer. He was just one of more than 200,000 men in the United States who learn they have the disease each year. Indeed, other than non-melanoma forms of skin cancer, prostate cancer is the most common cancer in American men. According to the American Cancer Association, one out of every six men will be diagnosed with the disease some time during their lives. Men are more likely to get prostate cancer than they are to get lymphoma, melanoma, colon, bladder, and kidney cancers combined. And, although an estimated 27,000 men die of the disease each year, many more survive. In fact, there are more than 2 million men living in the United States today who were diagnosed with the disease at some point in their lives

Lack of Knowledge

Knowing about prostate cancer is vital to surviving the disease. Yet many men do not know what factors put them at risk of developing the disease or what steps they can take to help prevent it. Nor do they understand the importance of early detection and treatment. Indeed, a 2006 Prostate Cancer Foundation survey of men throughout the United States found almost 33 percent of those surveyed did not know basic facts about the disease. This lack of knowledge is not limited to the United States. According to the Prostate Cancer Charity, a British prostate cancer advocacy organization, 90 percent of adults in the United Kingdom do not know what role the prostate gland plays in the body. "Most men," says prostate cancer expert Patrick Walsh, MD, "don't know they have a prostate until they have a problem from it."[1] Because prostate cancer does not usually produce symptoms until the disease has advanced, waiting until problems arise can reduce a man's chance of survival.

Well-known baseball manager Joe Torre, pictured here in 2007, battled prostate cancer in 1999.

Lowering Risk

Cancer experts all agree that diagnosing any form of cancer early, when it is most treatable, is vital to survival. In fact, if prostate cancer is diagnosed in an early stage before it has spread beyond the prostate, the five-year survival rate is 100 percent. Not only that, the cure rate is more than 90 percent. But, if the disease has already advanced, the five-year survival rate falls to 32 percent.

Fortunately, modern detection methods make it easy to monitor the status of a man's prostate, look for suspicious changes, and screen for the illness during routine annual physical exams. Thus, the disease can be detected when it is most treatable

That is what happened to Torre. He recalls:

It was a routine check-up and my doctor caught it through my PSA test [a blood test for a protein, which when it is elevated is associated with prostate cancer]. The key is men need to know that we can do something about prostate cancer but it starts with taking care of your health and getting your PSA checked especially if this disease is in your family or you're over 50. Don't be afraid of it. You can't get checked too soon, because even if your test indicates you don't have it, you can use your information to track and stay on top of your health.[2]

Stereotypes and Misconceptions

Despite the benefit of prostate cancer screening, many men do not bother to have a prostate exam. There are a number of reasons why this is so. One reason is that men are less likely to seek preventive medical care than women. In fact, only 40 percent of all doctor visits each year, whether due to a health problem or for prevention, are made by men. According to Leslie R Schover, professor of behavioral science at the University of Texas M.D. Anderson Cancer Center, Houston, "Men in our culture are brought up with the male stereotype to be strong, uncomplaining and tough. For many men, even an annual check-up is

Prostate health can be checked quite easily during a man's annual doctor visit, but many men are hesitant to go to the doctor for an exam in the first place.

a sign of weakness. Men may wait until a health emergency to see a doctor."[3] Most experts agree that despite cultural pressure, if men were more aware of what their prostate does, what can go wrong with it, and how early screening could save their lives, they would be more likely to go for such tests.

Another reason some men do not get checked is because the screening examination includes a rectal exam, which they mistakenly believe is painful. "Many men fear the rectal exam, but fear never dawned on me," explains prostate cancer survivor Raleigh Woodward. "I view it as a tool, part of an examination to help detect a disease in your body. If it's going to help find cancer, then why not do it?"[4]

Similarly, because of the nature of the exam, some men avoid it because they find it embarrassing or unmanly. But like all medical exams, it is administered in a professional manner and does not diminish an individual's masculinity. Being better informed about the test should help clear up these misconceptions. Prominent U.S. minister Louis Farrakhan, a prostate cancer survivor, explains: "We don't want a digital examination in our rectum. We feel that it's not manly. But we must have the exams. Go to your doctor. Don't even wait until you are 40, start at 35 to get digital exams and blood work. Think more about your health and the well-being of your bodies. It's imperative. You can't do that unless you change . . . your thinking."[5]

Becoming Aware

Learning about prostate cancer is the best way to get men to change their thinking and go for a prostate screening exam. Such knowledge can also help men learn what factors put them at risk of developing the disease and what steps they can take to lessen their chances of contracting the condition. For instance, maintaining a normal body weight and eating a healthy diet appear to help stave off the disease. And, if the disease is diagnosed, this knowledge can help men with prostate cancer and their loved ones to understand the challenges they face while giving them the information they need to make informed decisions about their treatment. Learning about prostate cancer today could save a man's life in the future. "Knowledge," explains author and prostate cancer expert Thomas Mawn, MD, "is indeed power . . . where life and its quality is concerned, ignorance should never be an excuse."[6]

CHAPTER ONE

What is Prostate Cancer?

Prostate cancer is a form of cancer that affects men. It develops in the prostate, a small, spongy, walnut-shaped gland that is part of the male reproductive system. The prostate gland is located in a man's pelvis, in front of the rectum and just below the bladder, the gland that stores urine. The urethra, a tube that transports urine and semen out of the body, runs through the prostate. On both sides of the prostate are nerves vital to a man's ability to achieve an erection. The prostate works in conjunction with the seminal vesicles, other reproductive organs attached to the prostate, to make seminal fluid or semen, the milky fluid that carries sperm out of the penis when a man ejaculates. The prostate needs the male sex hormone testosterone to function.

Prostate cancer develops when mutated prostate cells grow uncontrollably without purpose. Besides causing problems in the prostate, these cells can break away from the prostate and spread to other parts of the body where they can cause further damage. These characteristics, the uncontrolled and purposeless growth of cells, and the ability of those cells to spread throughout the body, define cancer.

Unlike normal cells, mutated cancer cells have no particular function other than dividing. And, because tumor suppressor genes play a role in signaling cell death, cancer cells do not die when they get old. So, if cancer is left unchecked, cancer cell growth can go on indefinitely. According to Robert A. Weinberg, the discoverer of the oncogene,

> The 30 trillion cells of the normal healthy body live in a complex interdependent condominium [mutually supporting network] . . . Normal cells reproduce only when instructed to do so . . . Such unceasing collaboration ensures that each tissue maintains the size and architecture appropriate to the body's needs. Cancer cells, in stark contrast, violate this scheme [plan]; they become deaf to the usual controls of proliferation [cell production] and follow their own internal agenda for reproduction.[8]

The Prostate

The prostate is located between the bladder and the penis, directly above the rectum. The prostate is enclosed in a capsule, a thin strong membrane. When prostate cancer spreads it escapes the capsule.

The prostate gland's function is to make semen, which it does in conjunction with the seminal vesicles, tiny organs located just behind the prostate. When a man has an orgasm, muscles squeeze semen from the prostate into the urethra, the tube that runs through the prostate. At the same time, sperm, which is produced in the testicles, also goes into the urethra. The two substances mix and the semen carries the sperm out through the penis.

The prostate is also involved in urination. The gland does not have an actual urinary function, but its location makes it important to the process. Besides carrying semen, the urethra carries urine out of the body. As a man ages and the prostate enlarges, it can press on the urethra, affecting urine flow.

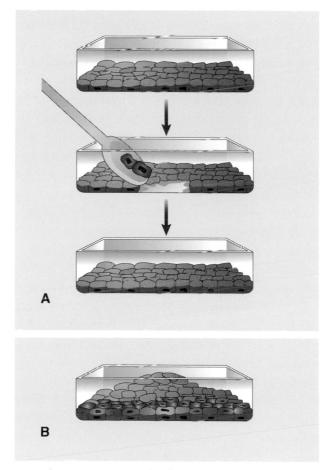

How a tumor forms: Normal cells divide to replace cells that have been scraped away (illustration A); cancer cells, on the other hand, pile up to form a tumor (illustration B).

A Tumor Forms

As the mutated cells keep dividing, they crowd together forming a mass known as a tumor. Tumors can be malignant or benign. Benign tumors are composed of normal cells that bump together. Because they consist of normal cells that do not grow uncontrollably, benign tumors are relatively harmless. A malignant tumor, on the other hand, is composed of mutated cells whose sole purpose is to divide. Consequently a malignant tumor keeps expanding in mass. As it does, it takes blood, oxygen, and nutrients away from nearby cells. This hampers the ability of normal cells to function and eventually destroys them.

This is not the only problem caused by a malignant tumor. As a malignant tumor grows in the prostate, it can block the outlet of the bladder inhibiting a man's ability to urinate. It can also press on the nerves that help a man have an erection causing erectile dysfunction, a term used to describe the inability to get or maintain an erection. "Cancer wreaks havoc . . . [Its] presence in human tissue signals chaos and a break down of normal function. Cancer brings unwelcome change to a biological machine that is perfect, marvelously beautiful and complex beyond measure,"[9] explains Weinberg.

A tumor large enough to cause a blockage in the prostate contains at least a billion cells. Malignant tumors start from one mutant cell that divides to form another cell, which divides, and so on. How fast a cancer cell divides is known as its doubling time, that is the time it takes for one cancer cell to divide and double. Some types of cancers, such as lung cancer, can double in less than a month. Prostate cancer is unpredictable. There are different types of prostate cancer, and men can have multiple types located in different parts of the gland. Some types are aggressive, doubling quickly. These include small cell and squamous cell carcinomas. But the most common type of prostate cancer, adenocarcinoma, is generally slow growing, taking about two years to double.

The Cancer Spreads

Even if a malignant tumor is not aggressive, it still poses a threat to the body. Normally when a harmful substance threatens the body, the immune system launches an attack. But cancer confounds the immune system. A malignant tumor is composed of mutated body cells. The immune system is programmed to attack foreign substances like bacteria or viruses, not body cells. Therefore, the tumor is left to grow undisturbed.

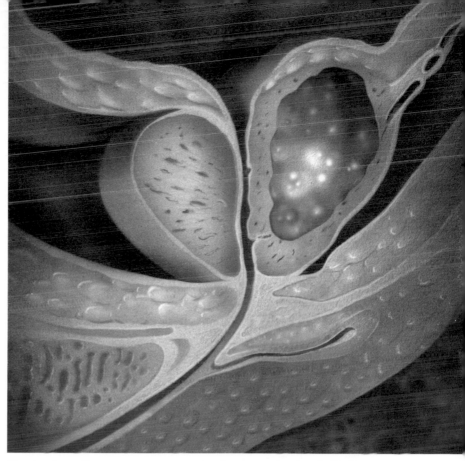

Illustration of a cancerous tumor in the prostate gland. If left unchecked, eventually cancer cells can break off from the tumor and enter the bloodstream, carrying cancerous cells to other parts of the body.

As the tumor expands, it can spread through the prostate and into neighboring tissue. Eventually, cancer cells can break off from the tumor and enter the bloodstream, or the lymphatic system, a network of thin tubes that carry white blood cells throughout the body. The cells are then transported to other organs, where they lodge themselves, grow, divide, and form new tumors. This is known as metastasis. Author and prostate cancer survivor F. Ralph Berberich, MD, has this to say about the process: "Cancer . . . emerges much like a pest that you swat, only to to see itrear its ugliness in another corner when you least expect it."[10]

Prostate cancer cells can spread anywhere, but they are most likely to metastasize in the bones. Slow growing prostate cancer can take twenty-five to thirty years to metastasize, while more aggressive cases can spread quickly. In either case, once prostate cancer metastasizes it eventually causes death.

Older Men at Risk

Although any man can develop prostate cancer, there are certain factors that put an individual at risk. The most significant is old age. Young men do get prostate cancer, and when they do for reasons that are not yet understood, it is more likely to be an aggressive form. But, in general, the disease rarely appears before age 40 and an individual's likelihood of developing prostate cancer sharply increases after age 50. For example, up to age 39, a man's odds of developing prostate cancer are 1 in 12,833. The odds rise significantly as a man ages, increasing to 1 in 2,500 at age 45, 1 in 476 at age 50, 1 in 120 at age 55, 1 in 43 at age 60, and 1 in 21 by age 65. David Nawrocki, a prostate cancer survivor, was in this last group. He remembers: "On a hot August day in 1997 . . . at the age of 62 . . . my urologist says, 'You've got an advanced case of prostate cancer.'"[11]

After a man reaches 65 years old, his risk rises even more sharply. By age 70, the odds jump to 1 in 9, and increase to 1 in 6 over the course of a lifetime. In fact, more than 65 percent of all prostate cancer cases are diagnosed in men over age 65, with the average age at the time of diagnosis being 70 years old. According to William Hyman, MD, of the Tyler Cancer Center, Tyler, Texas, "If all men lived long enough, you'd probably find some prostate problems arising."[12]

Scientists are not certain why age makes individuals more susceptible to the disease. They think it may be linked to the fact that, unlike other organs that cease growing when an individual reaches adulthood, for unknown reasons the prostate gland increases in size as a man ages. At birth the gland weighs less than 0.10 ounces (2.38g) and is about the size of a pea. Once puberty occurs the prostate grows to 0.33 ounces (9.36g). It increases to 0.50 ounces (15g), the size of a walnut, by the time a man reaches his mid-twenties. By age 50, the prostate weighs about 1 ounce (30 g) and keeps enlarging thereafter. How much

Exposure to Toxic Chemicals and Prostate Cancer

Besides the known risk factors that make an individual susceptible to prostate cancer, there are other factors that may put a man at risk. One is his occupation. Men who work with certain chemicals appear to have a higher risk of developing prostate cancer than other individuals. These include men who work with batteries and are exposed to cadmium, welders, farmers, and rubber plant workers. In addition, the United States government presumes that Vietnam War veterans who were exposed to the herbicide Agent Orange are also at greater risk. Accordingly, it provides these men special medical coverage. Although it is unclear whether these chemicals actually do cause prostate cancer, scientists do know that some chemicals, known as carcinogens, can promote cell mutation.

it grows varies from individual to individual. Although it is not common, prostates have been known to reach the size of an orange weighing in at 3 ounces (90g). Because the organ keeps growing, prostate cells divide often. The more frequently cells divide, the more chances they have to mutate and, scientists theorize, for cancer to develop.

Family History

A family history of prostate cancer also increases a man's vulnerability to developing the disease. People with a family history of the disease are genetically predisposed to developing it, which means that small differences in the genes that these individuals inherit from their parents increase their chances of developing prostate cancer. In fact, 42 percent of all prostate cancer cases are attributed to genetics. Steven, a prostate cancer survivor, explains how this affected his family: "Within 6 years, my father, 3 of my uncles, and 2 brothers were diagnosed with prostate cancer. I felt like I was on the railroad track with my foot stuck and I could see the train coming. Then I was diagnosed."[13]

An individual's risk rises with the number of family members that are affected, as well as the affected family member's relationship to that individual. For instance, if a man's father has had prostate cancer, that man is twice as likely to develop the disease as an individual with a healthy father. If a man's brother has had the condition, he is three times more likely to develop the disease than are men with healthy brothers. Due to this risk factor, prostate cancer survivor Frank Legacki was not surprised when he was diagnosed. He explains: "I'm the oldest of eight children, and there are six boys. I had two brothers who had prostate cancer before me, so I was on high alert. Now five of the six brothers have had prostate cancer."[14]

Moreover, if two or more first-degree family members have the disease, the man's risk rises five-fold. First-degree relatives include parents and siblings. If three or more relatives, including fathers, brothers, grandfathers, and uncles, have had the disease, a man's chance of developing prostate cancer jumps to almost 100 percent. Massachusetts senator John Kerry, former New York mayor Rudy Guiliani, and former Chicago Cubs and San Francisco Giants baseball team manager Dusty Baker are all prostate cancer survivors who fall into this category.

Additionally, there appears to be a link between a family history of breast cancer and prostate cancer, at least in African American men. A 2006 study in Flint, Michigan, tracked family history of cancer in 121 African American men with prostate cancer and 179 without prostate cancer. Besides being more likely to have a brother diagnosed with prostate cancer, the men with prostate cancer were four times more likely to have a sister diagnosed with breast cancer than the men who did not have prostate cancer. Researcher Kathleen Cooney, MD, explains: "Collecting a family history of prostate and breast cancer, especially among siblings, could be a key component of assessing prostate cancer risk . . . These findings give potential to identifying new genes associated with prostate and breast cancer."[15]

A family history of prostate cancer also affects the age of the disease's onset. Men with a family history of prostate cancer tend to develop the illness in their mid-fifties or younger. An estimated 65 percent of men diagnosed with the disease by age fifty-six have a family history of the disease. Dusty Baker, his uncle, and two grandfathers all had prostate cancer at an early age. He recalls:

> I never thought I had cancer in my family. My grandfather on both sides died in their 40s, and my uncle on my mom's side died in his mid-40s. But no one talked about why. After my prostate cancer diagnosis, my aunt sent me death certificates that showed the causes of death for my uncles and grandfather: prostate cancer. I had no idea— their cancers were never mentioned. My dad had been diagnosed with prostate cancer 8 years earlier, but I didn't know it affected my risk.[16]

Ethnicity

Race is another key risk factor. Among all ethnic groups, African Americans are the most vulnerable to prostate cancer. According to the Center for Disease Control and Prevention, African Americans have the highest rate of prostate cancer in the world. They are about 69 percent more likely to develop the condition than Caucasian men, the second largest group to develop the cancer. African Americans are also more likely to be diagnosed at a younger age. For example, 4.4 of every 100,000 Caucasian men in the United States between ages 40 to 45 are diagnosed with prostate cancer annually compared to13.2 African American males. Between ages 45 and 49, the incidence is 28.3 Caucasian males per 100,000 compared to 79.2 African American men. This disparity is even larger between ages 50 to 54 with 120.9 Caucasian men per 100,000 compared to 254.3 African Americans.

African American men also face a higher death rate from the disease. They are at least 50 percent more apt to die of the disease than other ethnic groups. "Prostate cancer, particularly among African Americans, is a . . . tragedy that needs immediate and drastic action,"[17] says John R. Kelly of the American Cancer Society.

The high death toll is partially due to the fact that the cancer tends to advance more rapidly in African Americans than it does in other ethnic groups. Scientists do not know why this is so. They theorize that there may be a genetic basis. African American males may carry a mutated gene or genes that not only predisposes them to developing prostate cancer, but also encourages prostate cancer growth.

A ten-year Harvard University study that ended in 2001 found one such genetic link, which may help explain why African Americans are more likely to develop aggressive prostate cancer. The study, which tracked the incidence of prostate can-

Among all ethnic groups, African Americans have the highest rate of prostate cancer in the world.

cer in more than forty-five thousand men of different ethnic groups, examined prostate cells taken from the men. All prostate cells contain androgen receptors, which produce a protein that binds with testosterone, the hormone prostate cells need to divide. The researchers found that the receptors of the African American subjects had a slight alteration. They theorized that the alteration causes the receptors to produce an excess amount of the protein, resulting in an increase in testosterone in the prostate. Since testosterone is required for prostate cell growth, by bringing more testosterone into the prostate, the protein indirectly aggravates cell division. The more rapidly cancer cells divide, the more aggressive the disease.

Another study conducted in 2003 at the Roswell Park Cancer Institute, Buffalo, New York, went a step further. It measured and compared the protein levels in prostate tissue samples of African American and Caucasian men, with and without prostate cancer. The protein was 22 percent higher in the benign tissue of the African Americans and 81 percent higher in the malignant tissue. Researcher James Mohler, MD, explains: "African-Americans suffer such disproportionately high death rates from prostate cancer compared to Caucasian-Americans . . . This study proves genetic differences may account for . . . these disparities."[18]

Lifestyle Factors

Other risk factors are less clear. Although there is no definitive proof, scientists and healthcare professionals think that certain lifestyle factors can raise an individual's prostate cancer risk. These include dietary factors and body weight.

A number of different studies have examined the link between lifestyle factors and prostate cancer. The studies tracked groups as large as seventy thousand men throughout the United States over periods as long as thirteen years, surveying their diet and weight, among other things. In study after study, researchers noticed a link between eating a high fat diet, rich in red meat, and prostate cancer. For instance, the previously mentioned Harvard study found that men who ate five or more servings

Lifestyle factors, such as being overweight, can raise an individual's prostate cancer risk.

of red meat per week were 79 percent more likely to develop prostate cancer than men who ate a diet lower in fat and red meat. The influence of other risk factors, however, was not considered in deriving these numbers. Consequently, scientists cannot say for sure whether a diet high in fat and red meat actually causes prostate cancer. They do, however, think it plays a role. They point to the fact that the incidence of prostate cancer and prostate cancer deaths vary from country to country with the highest rates occurring in North America and Scandinavia, parts of the world where fat and red meat consumption is high. The lowest rates occur in Asia, where little fat and red meat are consumed. Interestingly, when men from countries with a low incidence of prostate cancer move to the United States and adopt a western diet their prostate cancer rates increase. For example, the incidence of prostate cancer in Japan is 4 men per 100,000. The rate for Japanese men living in the United States is 20 per 100,000.

The studies also found a link between obesity and prostate cancer. Although the studies found that excess body weight does not appear to raise a man's risk of developing nonaggressive prostate cancer, it does raise his chances of developing and dying from an aggressive form of prostate cancer. Obesity also puts individuals at risk of having prostate cancer recur after prostate cancer surgery. Doctors do not know why obesity increases a man's risk of developing aggressive prostate cancer or experiencing a recurrence. Nevertheless, according to a 2002 University of California, San Francisco, study, the chance of recurrence for obese individuals is 70 percent higher than that for other prostate cancer patients. American Cancer Society scientist Carmen Rodriguez, MD, says: "Weight is one of the most common cancer risk factors that people have the ability to control . . . Emphasis should be put on the importance of avoiding weight gain to reduce the risk of prostate cancer."[19]

Clearly, risk factors like age, ethnicity, and genetics cannot be controlled. Lifestyle factors, on the other hand, can be. Although controlling these factors can improve an individual's general health, there is no guarantee such steps will prevent prostate cancer. "I had assumed myself to be a reasonably healthy man," explains writer and prostate cancer survivor Michael Korda. "I ate and drank moderately and I ran, worked out at the gym, or swam everyday. Now I had cancer."[20] Indeed, despite an individual's best efforts, if prostate cells mutate and grow uncontrollably, prostate cancer results.

CHAPTER TWO

Diagnosing Prostate Cancer

Since most cases of prostate cancer are slow growing, symptoms rarely appear early in the disease. A prostate cancer screening, which is a typical part of a routine physical examination for men, can detect a problem before symptoms appear. If a problem is detected, steps are taken to conclusively establish the presence of prostate cancer as well as to determine how advanced the disease may be.

Shared Symptoms

Prostate cancer symptoms usually do not arise until the tumor enlarges and causes a blockage, at which point the disease is likely to be advanced. Modern screening methods make it possible to detect prostate cancer before symptoms appear. As a matter of fact, most cases of prostate cancer are diagnosed in men who feel perfectly healthy. Michael Korda explains: "Prostate cancer creeps up on its victims silently, often striking men who appear to be 100 percent fit and healthy . . . The words most often heard by urologists [doctors who specialize in diseases of the urinary tract and male reproductive system] on informing a patient that he has prostate cancer are, 'But I have never felt better in my life.'"[21]

Even when prostate cancer symptoms do arise, since they are commonly associated with more benign prostate disorders that occur as men age and the prostate enlarges, they do

As men age, it is common for the prostate gland to enlarge causing symptoms such as difficulty urinating. Because many older men expect these symptoms, they may not recognize that prostate cancer can cause the same symptoms.

not raise an alarm. Because the urethra passes through the prostate, any problems in the prostate are likely to affect an individual's urinary functions. The most common prostate cancer symptoms include frequent urination especially at night, painful urination, difficulty passing urine, and/or a feeling of urgency when urinating. These symptoms are also an indicator of benign prostatic hyperplasia (BPH), a condition caused by hormonal changes that occur as a man ages. Such changes accelerate prostate growth, which causes the gland to constrict the urethra hindering urine flow. According to the National Institute of Health, BPH affects more than 50 percent of men age fifty-five and over, and more than 90 percent of those over seventy. Because most men expect these symptoms to arise as they age, they rarely take them seriously. Prostate cancer survivor William Martin, for example, did not think his symptoms were significant:

> I had always drunk large quantities of liquids, with the consequent need for frequent trips to the rest room. But about ten years ago, when I was still in my mid-forties, the interval between trips began to grow shorter and the urgency a bit more pressing. I was aware that this was a common side effect of aging, without knowing precisely why, and managed to take it with some good humor.[22]

Other prostate cancer symptoms are also often attributed to other conditions. Blood in the urine, another prostate cancer symptom, is found in bacterial infections such as a bladder infection or prostatitis, an inflammation of the prostate. While nonurinary symptoms like erectile dysfunction are frequently credited to diabetes, aging, and some sexually transmitted diseases. If the tumor encircles the rectum digestive symptoms such as constipation, abdominal pain, and intermittent diarrhea can occur. These are likely to be mistaken for irritable bowel syndrome.

As the cancer advances and spreads to the bones, pain in the hips and lower back are common. Again, because joint pain often occurs as an individual ages, such pain is frequently ascribed to old age, an injury, or arthritis. Similarly, general cancer symptoms such as fatigue and weakness are frequently mistaken for a sign of aging or the stress of daily life. Fatigue was Korda's only symptom and he disregarded it for over a year. He recalls: "I tried to think if there were any signs of cancer that I'd ignored . . . I could think of nothing significant, unless it was a certain amount of fatigue over the past year or so, a feeling that I tired more easily than in the past and needed more rest."[23]

Diagnosis Based on Screening

Since prostate cancer does not produce clear symptoms, most cases are detected during a physical examination when a prostate screening is administered. Such screening begins with a digital (or finger) examination of the patient's rectum. During a digital rectal exam (DRE), the patient bends forward over the examining table or lies sideways on the table with his knees pulled up close to his chest. Then, the doctor gently inserts a gloved and lubricated finger through the patient's anus into the rectum. In this manner, the doctor can feel through the rectal wall to the back of the prostate gland where it is in contact with the rectum. Normally, the prostate is smooth. Bumps, nodules, or rough spots all can be a sign of cancer, or may be caused by a benign tumor or scar tissue. The exam, which is not painful but can cause an uncomfortable burning sensation, takes only a minute or two. Famed photographer, explorer, and prostate

During a digital rectal exam the doctor gently inserts a gloved and lubricated finger through the patient's anus into the rectum. The doctor can feel through the rectal wall to the back of the prostate gland where it is in contact with the rectum.

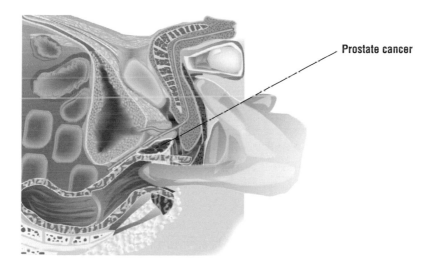

Prostate cancer

cancer survivor Charles Neider's cancer was first detected via a digital rectal exam. He recalls that the doctor

> Gave me a prolonged and vigorous digital rectal exam, which the physician performs with a lubricated latex-gloved finger. . . . As most men would probably agree, this is an embarrassing procedure at best. At times, it can make you very uncomfortable . . . After getting dressed I went to his office . . . [The doctor said] there may be a suspicious protuberance [lump] in my prostate.[24]

A PSA Test

A digital rectal exam is good for detecting abnormalities in the rear peripheral zone of the prostate, the most common site for prostate tumors to develop. If a tumor is located in the middle or front of the prostate, areas that cannot be reached easily via a digital examination, it will probably not be detected. And, early-stage tumors are often too small to be felt. To solve these problems, a prostate specific antigen (PSA) blood test is also administered. It involves drawing blood from a vein in a patient's arm. It can detect early stage tumors throughout the gland. Andy Grove, a prostate cancer survivor and former chief executive officer of Intel explains: "Typically, a PSA test can indicate the presence of prostate cancer as much as five years earlier than diagnosis by other means, like digital rectal exam . . . Since the PSA test accelerates the discovery of the tumor in the first place, you have the chance to treat tumors earlier than ever before."[25]

PSA is a protein made in the prostate gland. Its function is to liquefy semen. Both normal and cancerous prostate cells produce PSA. The more rapidly prostate cells divide, the more PSA that is produced. Normally, only small amounts of PSA are found in the bloodstream. Abnormalities of the prostate, which cause prostate cells to divide more frequently, can cause PSA to leak into the bloodstream and raise PSA blood levels.

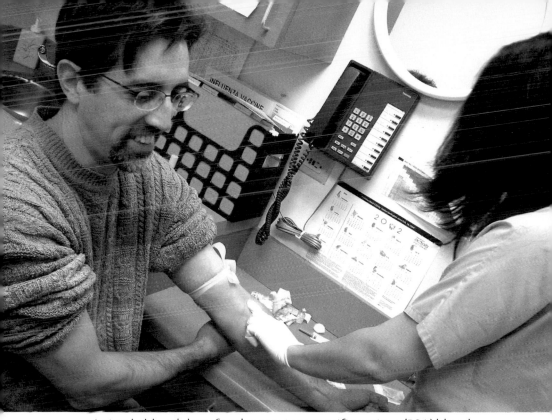

A simple blood draw for the prostate specific antigen (PSA) blood test can detect early stage prostate tumors.

PSA is measured in nanograms (ng/ml), or billionths of a gram per milliliter of blood, and can be anywhere from 0 to 1,000 or more. Levels of 4 ng/ml or less are considered normal. Elevated levels raise suspicions of prostate cancer. The higher the level, the more likely the cause is prostate cancer. For example, when PSA levels are between 4 and 10, a man has a 25 percent chance of the cause being prostate cancer. Above 10, the chance of prostate cancer climbs to 50 percent. Moreover, a very high PSA level, above 20, for example, often indicates the presence of a large tumor that may have spread beyond the prostate.

Although a PSA test is a very valuable diagnostic tool, like most medical tests it is not perfect. For unknown reasons, one out of every five men with prostate cancer do not have elevated PSA. John B. was one of these men. He remembers: "Although my PSA was low, during a DRE my prostate felt firm to my doctor, so I underwent a biopsy. My urologist, my wife, and I were shocked when the biopsy showed cancer."[26]

Moreover, prostatitis and BPH, conditions that cause faster than normal cell division, also cause PSA levels to rise. And, for unexplained reasons, some men with normal prostates have high PSA. Indeed, fifteen out of every one hundred men age fifty or older have abnormal PSA levels, yet only three are diagnosed with prostate cancer. Berberich explains:

> The PSA can give false positive and false negative results. Men whose PSA is elevated may have a normal or noncancerous prostate, while men whose PSA is normal may nevertheless have cancer. To make matters even more confusing, the PSA also rises with age, the size of the prostate gland, prostate inflammation, and a common noncancerous enlargement called BPH.[27]

That is why if a man's PSA is slightly elevated, but the digital rectal exam does not detect any abnormalities, many doctors do not proceed with other more invasive diagnostic procedures immediately. Instead, they monitor the patient's PSA velocity, that is, how fast the patient's PSA rises, over a course of twelve to eighteen months. This involves repeatedly testing and tracking PSA levels. In general, since cancerous cells divide more rapidly than normal cells, blood levels of PSA increase at a greater rate due to prostate cancer than from other less serious conditions. It is not uncommon for PSA levels of individuals with prostate cancer to more than double within a year. And, even if an individual's PSA was previously within the normal range, a rise of more than 0.75 ng/ml in a year is a red flag that further diagnostic steps are needed.

Monitoring Bert Gottleib's PSA velocity led to his diagnosis. Gottleib recalls:

> It was the twenty-first of February, 1994, at the second report visit of my annual physical and I wasn't listening all that hard. I felt strong and energetic and besides, was

accustomed to, and fully expected to hear, "Your heart's strong, lungs are clear, blood pressure is that of a twenty-year old," the usual. But as I was reaching down to pick up my bag, ready to dash, Doctor Dominguez looked up from his reports and said, "Your PSA's doubled . . . I don't like that."[28]

Despite its flaws, PSA testing can save lives. Prostate cancer survivor Bob Russell agrees: "It's a way of starting the

PSA

PSA is a relatively recent discovery, and an even newer screening tool for prostate cancer. Prostate cancer expert Paul H. Lange, MD, discusses how it became a screening tool:

> Prostate specific antigen (PSA) was first discovered in the 1970s by several researchers in Japan and the United States. It wasn't actually named until 1979, when Dr. Ming Wang described PSA in an article in Investigative Urology. In 1980, Dr. Wang created a blood test for PSA. The Food and Drug Administration (FDA) began approving PSA blood tests in 1985. The test was initially approved for determining whether anticancer therapies were working in men who already were being treated with prostate cancer. My colleagues and I were fortunate enough to be very involved in these early studies. In 1990 and 1991, several groups, including mine, discovered and published that PSA was also effective in screening and diagnosis. . . . Today PSA is the definitive test for detecting early prostate cancer in the United States and other countries.

Paul H. Lange, MD, and Christine Adamec, *Prostate Cancer for Dummies*. New York: Wiley, 2003.

process, of seeing whether you are one of the ones that are perhaps unlucky, but you may have prostate cancer, and if you do something about it in a timely fashion, you can beat it. If you don't, it's going to beat you."[29]

From Detection to Diagnosis

A prostate cancer screening exam is, indeed, merely the start of the prostate cancer diagnosis process. Even when the results point to cancer, neither a digital rectal examination nor a PSA blood test can conclusively determine whether the problem is prostate cancer or if the cause is a less threatening condition. And, if cancer is present, these tests cannot establish the aggressiveness of the cancer. The only way to make these determinations is via a biopsy. That is a procedure in which at least six to fourteen samples of prostate tissue are removed and sent to a laboratory, where a specialized doctor known as a pathologist

A doctor discusses the results of a prostate ultrasound with her patient. The ultrasound can provide the physician with images of surrounding body parts to see whether the cancer has spread beyond the prostate gland.

studies the samples under a microscope in order to establish whether the cells are normal or cancerous.

A prostate biopsy is administered in conjunction with a transrectal ultrasound (TRUS), which is used to guide the biopsy needles. An ultrasound is a procedure that utilizes high frequency sound waves, which bounce off body tissues to create echo patterns. A computer translates the patterns into images of the body part being examined, which are displayed on a video monitor. Tumors produce different echo patterns than healthy body tissue.

A TRUS is usually performed in a hospital as an outpatient procedure by a urologist, assisted by a specially trained technician. During a TRUS, patients lay on an examining table on their side with their knees against their chest. A small probe, a little larger and wider than an adult's index finger, is gently inserted through the anus into the individual's rectum. The device, which emits sound waves, is lubricated and covered with a condom. The probe is moved around the prostate producing images on a video monitor of different parts of the gland. By studying these images, the urologist can ascertain whether a tumor is indeed present. And if it is, pinpoint its exact location. Then, using the video image as a guide, the doctor uses a gun-like device to insert narrow needles through the wall of the rectum into the prostate gland to extract tissue samples from the tumor as well as from other areas of the gland where the tumor may have spread. Thomas Mawn, MD, explains:

> Guided by the ultrasound image . . . When the physician has everything lined up, he can aim the tip of the biopsy needle and squeeze the trigger, confident he's on target. Once fired, a small needle shoots through the rectal wall (where there are few nerve endings to register pain) and springs back with a small core of tissue approximately one millimeter [0.04 inches] thick—enough for a pathologist to examine for abnormalities.[30]

In addition, TRUS can provide the physician with images and tissue samples of surrounding body parts such as the bladder and seminal vesicles. This allows the doctor to see whether the cancer has spread beyond the prostate gland.

The procedure takes about fifteen minutes. Although it is not painful, it can cause discomfort. Patients may be given oral pain medication, or the rectum may be numbed with an injection of an anesthetic to help relieve any discomfort. Gottleib describes his experience:

> It is indeed uncomfortable, but not painful . . . They [the doctor and technician] are all [in] concentration, guiding the probe, whispering words to each other as if announcing a golf game on TV. "This may sting a bit," Doctor Mawn warns my backside. The probe is twisted and turned until both seem happy with what they see on the video monitor, and then there's a tiny sharp bite deep inside me. Some fussing over slides. More probe wiggling and whispering. Then another bite. Then more. And now the doctor is helping me into a sitting position . . . I let out a breath I hadn't realized I'd been holding.[31]

Grading and Staging

If the biopsy reveals the presence of prostate cancer, the pathologist carefully examines the cancer cells to determine the type, grade, and stage of the cancer. The grade identifies the aggressiveness of the cancer cells. The stage refers to the location of the cells. Establishing these factors affects a patient's treatment options and his prognosis. That is an estimate of how likely the patient is to be cured, or his chances for long-term survival.

Grading prostate cancer helps to forecast how rapidly the cancer is apt to grow and spread. Prostate cancer cells are graded by how closely they resemble normal prostate cells. Those that look most like normal cells are said to be well-differentiated and are usually slow growing. Those that look very

A Bone Scan

If it is suspected that prostate cancer has spread to the bones, individuals are given a radionuclide whole-body bone scan. In this procedure, patients are injected in an arm vein with a harmless radioactive fluid, which washes over the bones and acts as a tracer. Then, the patient lays on a bed, similar to an examining table, and a machine much like an X-ray machine passes over and under him taking pictures. Cancer cells absorb the radioactive substance and appear as dark spots in the pictures. The procedure takes about a half-hour and is painless. The radioactive fluid quickly passes from the body in an individual's urine. Patients are advised to drink a lot of water before and after the procedure to help the fluid pass from the body.

different from normal cells are said to be poorly differentiated and are likely to develop quickly.

The system used to grade prostate cancer is called the Gleason grading system. Gleason grades ranges from 1 to 5. Cells that look most like normal cells, and are, therefore, least aggressive, are graded lowest, and those that look less normal are graded higher. To get a Gleason score, the pathologist grades cell samples taken from two areas of the prostate, and each sample is given a grade. The first grade is for the primary or most commonly seen cancer cells. The second grade is for the secondary or second most commonly seen cells. Then the two grades are written in the form of an equation, such as $1 + 3$, with the primary grade first and the secondary grade next, and added together to get a sum anywhere between 2 and 10. Scores ranging from 2 to 4 represent what is usually slow growing cancer. Scores between 5 and 7 are usually mildly aggressive. Scores over 7 usually indicate aggressive prostate cancer. But Gleason scores are not exact predictors. And, not all Gleason scores are the same. A Gleason score of 2 + 5 means that the most commonly seen cancer cells were graded 2, while a score of 5 + 2 indicates the most commonly seen cancer cells were graded 5. So, even though the final score of 7 is the same, a man whose case is scored 2 + 5 has more well-differentiated and therefore more slow growing cells than one scored 5 + 2.

Once the grade is established, the pathologist identifies the cancer stage. That is, the size and location of the tumor and whether it has spread. Examining cells taken from different parts of the prostate lets the pathologist make this assessment. Prostate cancer is divided into four stages, stage I, II, III, and IV. In stage I, the tumor is so small it cannot be felt during a digital rectal exam and has not spread outside the prostate. In stage II, the cancer is still contained within the prostate but involves more tissue than stage I. By stage III, the tumor begins to extend to tissue outside the prostate. Stage IV indicates the cancer has spread to any or all of these areas: the lymph nodes, the walls of the pelvis, tissue in the rectum and bladder, and/or the bones.

Making a Prognosis

Once the Gleason grade and stage of cancer is established, the doctor uses this information, plus the patient's PSA, level to make a prognosis. It is based on statistics of how well other patients of the same age, in similar general health, with the same PSA level, grade, and stage of cancer fared. Generally, patients in stage I or II, with a Gleason score between 2 and 6, and PSA less than 11 have the best prognosis. These patients usually are cured. Those in stages III or IV, with a Gleason score between 8 and 10, and PSA of 20 or more have a poorer prognosis.

However, a prognosis is not absolute. Cancer does not always act or respond as expected, and ongoing research may result in new treatments that can change everything. No matter the prognosis, once prostate cancer is diagnosed, graded, and staged, steps can be taken to increase a man's chance of long-term survival. "When I was diagnosed, my Gleason score was 7 plus," explains prostate cancer survivor John D. who is doing well despite an unfavorable prognosis. "I started out from the standpoint of, you know, 'You're really in bad shape. Where are we going from here?'"[32]

CHAPTER THREE

Treating Prostate Cancer

Once a diagnosis is made, treatment can begin. There are a variety of treatments for prostate cancer including surgery, radiation therapy, and hormone therapy, which can be administered separately or in combination. And, some patients choose to avoid active treatment and simply monitor slow-growing cases instead. Which method is best depends on the individual and the stage of the cancer.

Making a Decision

In general, after a diagnosis is made, the doctor provides prostate cancer patients with information about their treatment options. Although physicians may offer an opinion, it is up to the patient to choose his own treatment path. Berberich recalls his experience:

> At the end of the meeting, he [the doctor] laid out an array of therapy options including surgery; . . . external beam radiation alone, at a variety of doses and by a variety of different techniques, . . . external beam radiation, prostate or whole pelvis, plus radioactive seeds; short-term hormone administration plus radiation; and watchful waiting. The last possibility was the only one he immediately dismissed as unwise. He felt that a cure . . . was still a strong possibility and I should go for it. When I stated that I did

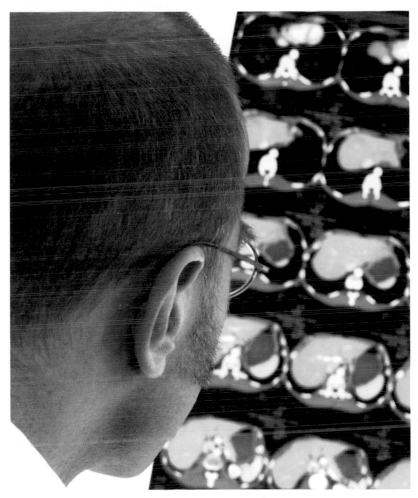

After a diagnosis is made, the doctor provides prostate cancer patients with information about their treatment options. Which method is best depends on the individual and the stage of the cancer.

not see surgery as the best choice, he did not object. I left feeling somewhat encouraged, my head spinning from the various choices and possible treatment combinations dumped in my vulnerable lap.[33]

Because long-term survival rates do not vary widely between most prostate cancer treatments and each method presents advantages and disadvantages, making a decision can be confusing and difficult. Individuals find that educating themselves about each form of treatment is the best way to ease this process. Consulting with medical specialists, doing research, and talking to other men who have undergone the various treatments all help. Thomas Sellers, a prostate cancer survivor, spoke with at least four different physicians before selecting a treatment plan. But that was not all he did. He explains:

> I was very aggressive in going out and getting additional information and second opinions. I talked to prostate cancer survivors to get the firsthand experience. I went to the American Cancer Society Web site and looked at all that information. It was through all of that, that I was able to put together enough information to feel comfortable and to really inform my decision.[34]

Fortunately, since most prostate cancer cases progress relatively slowly, it is usually safe for men with nonaggressive prostate cancer to take time to explore their options without the risk of the cancer spreading before treatment begins. Prostate cancer survivor, Don, is glad he did not hurry. He explains: "After diagnosis, having heard many myths about prostate cancer and treatment side effects, I decided to take my time making a decision and spent months researching. I don't necessarily recommend delaying a decision, but I do advocate educating yourself to all the facts before you decide. It's a very personal decision. No one should be making it for you."[35]

Surgery

After careful consideration, about 192,000 prostate cancer patients a year opt to have a radical prostatectomy. It is a type of surgery that involves the removal of the entire prostate gland, the seminal vesicles, and sometimes near-by pelvic lymph glands, if necessary. The surgery is considered the "gold-standard" for curing cancer contained in the prostate. In fact, ten-year survival and cure rates after a radical prostatectomy

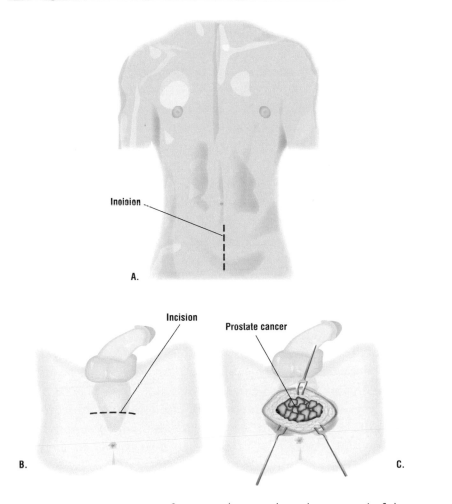

Incision

A.

Incision

Prostate cancer

B.

C.

A prostatectomy is a type of surgery that involves the removal of the entire prostate gland. The doctor makes a 4 to 6 inch incision either in the patient's lower abdomen (illustration A) or in his perenium, the area between the anus and genitals (illustration B). The prostate is then carefully detached from the urethra and bladder, and removed from the body.

top 95 percent. According to prostate cancer experts Paul H. Lange, MD, and Christine Adamec, "The benefit of the radical prostatectomy is that it often stops the cancer cold in its tracks. If the cancer hasn't spread beyond your prostate, and the cancerous growth is removed, the cancer cells will no longer be around to grow and attack the rest of the body. As a result, the prostatectomy cures your cancer."[36]

A radical prostatectomy is performed by a surgeon who specializes in urology. It takes about four hours and typically requires a four-day hospital stay. Before the operation begins, the patient is either sedated, or given a spinal injection, which numbs the lower half of his body. Then, the doctor makes a 4 to 6 inch (10.6 to 15.24cm) incision either in the patient's lower abdomen or in his perineum, the area between the anus and genitals. The prostate is then carefully detached from the urethra and bladder, and removed from the body. Because of the prostate's proximity to the two bundles of nerves that run alongside the prostate and control a man's ability to have an erection, this is a very delicate operation. In one specific type of radical prostatectomy known as nerve-sparing radical prostatectomy, the doctor makes every effort to avoid damaging these nerves. Most of the time, the doctor is successful. "My surgery proceeded without any complications and the specialist said it had been successful," explains Joe Torre. "In addition to getting all the cancer out, he was able to save both nerves on the prostate that control sexual function."[37] Unfortunately, sometimes because of the size or location of the tumor, this is not possible. Moreover, if the cancer has spread to the nerve bundles, one or both are removed.

Once the prostate is removed, the bladder opening is sewn onto the urethra. A rubber tube, known as a Foley catheter, is then passed through the penis into the bladder. Until the bladder and urethra heal, the tube is used to drain urine out of the body. This takes between one to two weeks.

Help from a Robot

Because the large incision wound can be quite painful, during their hospital stay patients are given intravenous pain medication. The wound usually takes about five weeks to heal, which can make a radical prostatectomy hard on patients. A new type of prostate surgery known as a laparoscopic radical prostatectomy (LPR), which does not require a large incision, offers patients another surgical option. Since it is less invasive than a traditional prostatectomy, both the length of the hospital stay and healing time are reduced.

In this procedure, the doctor's hands never enter the patient's body. Instead, the surgeon makes five keyhole size incisions in the patient's abdomen. A telescopic lens called a laparoscope is inserted in one incision. It takes three-dimensional pictures of the prostate that are transmitted to a computer monitor. Tiny surgical tools, which are connected to a robotic arm, are inserted through the other incisions. Using the images on the monitor as a guide, the doctor uses a joystick to manipulate the robotic arm and remove the prostate. As with traditional surgery, the urethra and bladder are sewn together and a Foley

Prostate cancer surgery has a high success rate, but there are side effects associated with it. Doctors and patients must weigh the side effects and decide what is the best course of action.

catheter is inserted, but these tasks are done robotically. Because this type of surgery has been in use for less than ten years, it is not available everywhere. But when it is used, cure rates equal those of traditional surgery. And, many patients are happy with the results. Pete is one such individual. He explains:

> The surgery took place on January 18, 2005 at about 8:30 in the morning. When I awakened in the recovery room at about 2:30 in the afternoon, I was uncomfortable, but not in great pain. There were five small incisions . . . and

The Prostate Cancer Team

There are a number of healthcare professionals involved in caring for prostate cancer patients. These include a family doctor or internist who administers the initial prostate cancer screening and an urologist who specializes in diseases of the prostate. A urologist often administers hormone therapy. Or, an oncologist, a doctor who specializes in the care of all types of cancer, may do this. In addition, urologists monitor patients who opt for expectant management.

A surgeon who specializes in urology performs a prostatectomy. In the hospital, nurses, technicians, and nurse's assistants care for the patient. And, a pain management team of physicians and nurses helps patients deal with pain after surgery.

A radiation oncologist is a doctor who specializes in treating cancer with radiation. He or she maps out radiation treatment, which is usually administered by radiation technicians and nurses. Specialized technicians also assist in administering imaging tests such as a TRUS.

In addition, prostate cancer patients also may be seen by counselors and mental health professionals to help them deal with emotional issues.

a Foley catheter had been inserted into my penis. That
night I had the some nausea and discomfort, but I was
able to get up and sit in a chair for a couple of hours and
then took a walk around the nurse's station. The following
afternoon I was released from the hospital . . . Five days
later I returned to the doctor's office where my catheter
was removed. That was a big relief and once the catheter
was gone, I recovered rapidly. One week after the operation I was able to get back to my walking program and by
three weeks I was walking over 2 miles each day.[38]

Risk Factors

Despite the high cure rate, both types of prostate surgery are
not without side effects. All operations carry the threat of
infection. In addition, if the bundle of nerves that run alongside the prostate are removed or damaged during surgery, erectile dysfunction results. Estimates for the incidence of erectile
dysfunction after prostate surgery is about 30 percent. Even if
there is no permanent nerve damage, it takes between three
months to a year after surgery for men to regain their ability to
have and maintain an erection. When they do, since their prostate has been removed they are no longer producing seminal
fluid and are no longer able to father a child.

Another problem is incontinence, the unintentional passing
of urine, which results in leakage or dribbling of urine. There
are two reasons for this. First, the prostate's location near the
bladder and the urinary sphincter, the valve that controls urine
flow by squeezing the urethra shut, can lead to trouble. The surgeon must remove the prostate without damaging the urinary
sphincter, which sometimes is not possible. Second, the prostate helps the urinary sphincter to control urine flow. Once the
gland is removed the job falls solely to the urinary sphincter. It
can take months for the body to adjust, and until it does surgical patients lack urinary control. And 5 to 10 percent of men
who have had a prostatectomy have long-term problems.

Despite these potential problems, many men feel that the benefits of prostate surgery outweigh the risks. Seven years after his surgery, Thomas Sellers is satisfied. "It's gotten progressively better over time," he explains. "I made the right choice for me, given my age, and the associate risks and benefits."[39]

Radiation Therapy

Radiation therapy is another treatment option for both early and advanced prostate cancer. It uses high-energy rays such as X-rays or protons to change the structure of cancer cells so that they can no longer divide. This causes the cells to die when they attempt to divide.

There are two main types of radiation therapy for prostate cancer, external and internal beam radiation therapy. Patients

Conformal radiation therapy uses computers to focus beams of radiation at the prostate, or other specific area of the body being treated. Pictured here is a patient undergoing conformal radiation therapy for a brain tumor.

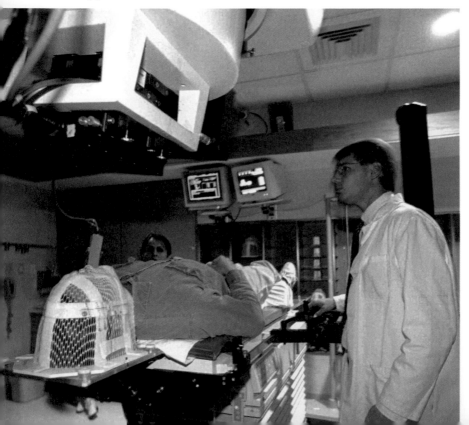

may receive one or both forms of treatment. In external beam radiation, beams of radiation are directed at the prostate gland by external machines. Since radiation also damages normal cells, every effort is made to ensure that the beams are precisely focused so that only the infected area is treated. With this in mind, a new form of radiation therapy known as three-dimensional conformal therapy, which uses computers to aim beams of radiation at the prostate from different angles, is increasingly being used.

Before treatment begins, the doctor, known as a radiation oncologist, uses imaging tools to see inside the prostate. Then, with the assistance of a computer, the doctor measures the correct angles to aim the radiation beams. Once this is determined, the patient's skin is marked with ink dots that will be used for focusing the radiation to the affected area. At the same time, a plastic mold is made of the patient's body. It acts like a cocoon, keeping the patient from moving during treatment. These precautions make it easier to deliver the radiation to the affected area without damaging near-by organs.

The therapy itself is painless. It is usually administered five days a week for seven to nine weeks in five to fifteen minute sessions. During these sessions, patients lay inside their body molds on a bed similar to an examining table. Above the bed is a machine much like an X-ray machine, which moves around the bed delivering radiation to the treatment field. Judy Eberhardt describes her husband's experience:

> Charlie was scheduled to undergo 40 radiation treatments, five days a week. We weren't alone: A gaggle of men, accompanied by their wives, shuffled in and out of the facility for their 15 minute treatments. Each man had his own "body pod" to climb into, before being zapped by a beam calibrated just for him . . . Charlie came through the treatment with flying colors![40]

Alternative Complementary Treatments

Some prostate cancer patients supplement conventional prostate cancer treatment with alternative treatments. Unlike traditional treatments, alternative treatments have not undergone rigorous testing to prove their safety and effectiveness. Nor, does the Federal Drug Administration (FDA), a government agency that sets standards and regulates approved treatments, regulate them. But many healthcare professionals say that combining such treatments with traditional treatment can help strengthen patients and lower their stress levels.

Popular complementary treatments include nutritional supplements to strengthen the body, as well as acupuncture, which involves the insertion of thin needles in certain points on the body to relieve pain. Yoga and tai chi, gentle forms of exercise that strengthen the body and calm the mind, are also popular.

Visualization and meditation are also popular. They use the mind to calm the body and promote healing. While meditating, individuals recite a word or phrase in an effort to calm the mind. During visualization, individuals envision mental images of their bodies healing.

Brachytherapy

Brachytherapy, or internal beam radiation, is administered differently. In this treatment, a urologist injects forty to one hundred radioactive pellets, each about the size of a grain of rice, directly into the patient's prostate. Using an ultrasound image as a guide to the location of the tumor, the physician positions a number of long thin hollow needles loaded with the seeds in the patient's perineum, the area between the anus and the genitals. When the seeds are implanted the needles are withdrawn.

Brachytherapy is done as an outpatient procedure in a hospital. Patients are usually given a spinal anesthetic to prevent any discomfort. Although it is not unusual to feel sore afterwards, patients can resume their normal activities as soon as they are released from the hospital. The radioactive seeds can be high or low dose. High dose pellets work quickly and are removed after a few days. Low dose pellets remain in the prostate indefinitely, but they lose their radioactivity in about three months. While they are still radioactive, patients are warned to take special care around pregnant women and young children, but in general the pellets are not a danger to others. Berberich recalls his experience: "I was lying on my left side and my back was being cleansed. I barely felt the needle poke . . . becoming numb from the waist down . . . I heard coordinates being shouted out and acknowledged . . . It was all over in about half an hour . . . I had been poked twenty-fives times with long needles that contained over a hundred radioactive pellets."[41]

Ten-year survival and cure rates for both types of radiation therapy are much the same as for surgery. Similarly, these therapies, too, present health risks. During treatment, individuals report problems such as diarrhea, rectal pain, incontinence, and abnormal urinary frequency. External radiation also causes extreme fatigue.

Although these issues usually ease when treatment ends, there can be long-term problems. About one out of three prostate cancer patients who receive radiation therapy continue to contend with frequent urination. Five percent of brachytherapy patients experience long-term bowel problems. And, although erectile dysfunction rarely occurs right after radiation therapy ceases, it sometimes occurs years later when scar tissue forms on the nerves around the prostate, affecting about 30 percent of all patients.

Paul Patrick, a prostate cancer survivor, experienced some of these problems while he underwent external radiation therapy. But today he is cancer free. "When you weigh it, the risk and the reward," he explains, "it's really not that big a deal."[42]

Hormone Therapy

Hormone therapy or androgen deprivation therapy, as it is also known, is yet another treatment option. Its goal is to lower testosterone levels, the hormone that is responsible for the growth of both normal and abnormal prostate cells. Depriving the body of testosterone shrinks and/or slows the growth of prostate cancer cells. Unless it is combined with radiation, hormone therapy cannot cure prostate cancer. But it can significantly slow the cancer process for a number of years, and it is effective in 85 to 95 percent of all cases in which it is administered. It is most appropriate for men for whom radiation or surgery are not good options due to their age or other health issues. It is also an option for men with metastatic prostate cancer, since the therapy works on prostate cancer cells no matter where they are located in the body.

Hormone therapy involves the administration of any number of medications, including the female hormone estrogen, which prevent the production of testosterone. Hormone therapy is administered via monthly injection, in pill form, or a combination of both. Treatment can go on indefinitely, but for unknown reasons, it often ceases to have a beneficial effect over time. Experts are testing whether administering the therapy when an individual's PSA rises and stopping it when it is declines will solve this problem.

Intermittent hormone therapy may also help lessen the side effects, which include hot flashes, greatly diminished sex drive, erectile dysfunction, loss of muscle mass and bone density, weight gain, fatigue, mood swings, irritability, and depression. Eighty-nine-year-old Charles Jenning started intermittent hormone therapy when he was eighty-two. Despite the side effects, he is doing well and does not have any prostate cancer symptoms. He explains: "I do feel I made the right choice for me. I don't have any reason to think I should have done anything else."[43]

Expectant Management

Other prostate cancer patients do not think any form of active treatment is the right choice for them. Their age, general health, or the risk of unpleasant side effects leads them to opt for expectant management instead. It involves monitoring, rather than actively treating, prostate cancer. The method, which is also known as watchful waiting, is based on the idea that because prostate cancer is usually slow growing, it is possible for men with nonaggressive prostate cancer to refuse active treatment and still live out their lives without the cancer causing any symptoms.

Expectant management is most appropriate for older individuals diagnosed with low grade and low stage prostate cancer, as well as for those individuals in poor general health who are too weak to endure other treatments. Typically, patients who opt for expectant management are given a digital rectal exam every six months, a PSA blood test every three months, and a TRUS once a year. If these tests detect any problems, other forms of treatment may be started. But, sometimes treatment can come too late and the cancer may have spread, which is a risk taken by individuals who select expectant management. "Watchful waiting was the best selection because of my age and strong desire to maintain the . . . lifestyle I have, which I treasure," explains seventy-nine-year-old John Sosdian. "I feel so good about what I am doing. I . . . have no concern if cancer should metastasize, resulting in my death."[44]

Clearly, every form of prostate cancer treatment has its advantages and disadvantages. Men with the disease must choose the treatment that they feel is right for them and then live with the consequences. Michael Korda, who experienced some health problems after a radical prostatectomy and a long recovery period, puts it this way: "Really when I think back on it, I got off lightly. Nine months of disruption, discomfort, and fear, followed by what has been so far a clean bill of health— I'm a lucky man."[45]

CHAPTER FOUR

Living with Prostate Cancer

Men with prostate cancer face physical and emotional challenges. The disease can take a toll on their bodies and raise emotional issues, as can the side effects of treatment. By taking steps to meet these challenges, individuals can improve the quality of their lives. The late singer Robert Goulet, who was a prostate cancer survivor himself, put it this way: "When you or the person you love is diagnosed with cancer, the first thought is of the end. . . . but I'm here to talk about the value of living with cancer. It's not an easy battle, but we need to believe life goes on even in the face of cancer, and life can become more full because of cancer."[46]

Overcoming Urinary Problems

Men with prostate cancer often face urinary problems. Those who have undergone prostate surgery must urinate through a catheter until the reconnected bladder and urethra heal. The catheter is attached to a bag, which is taped to the patient's leg and collects urine.

Managing the catheter and urine bag takes special knowledge. Before being released from the hospital, patients are instructed in how to remove the catheter for showering, clean the catheter and the area around the penis where the tube is inserted, empty the urine bag, and reinsert the catheter. Korda recalls:

The bag had to be emptied . . . The catheter tube also had to be cleaned at frequent intervals, sterilized with alcohol pads and coated with Neomycin [antibiotic] ointment. The penis and the first couple of inches of the tube as it emerged from the urethra then had to be wrapped with a surgical gauze pad, over which an absorbent pad was rolled. I was urged to watch this procedure carefully, as I would soon be doing it myself.[47]

To make dealing with the urine bag easier, patients are given two different size bags—a small bag for daytime use, and a large one for use at night. Using the large bag at night allows individuals to get a good night's rest without having to repeatedly get up to empty the bag. Putting a leak-proof mattress cover or rubber backed pads on the bed also helps individuals cope with the possibility of leakage during the night.

Those who have undergone prostate surgery must urinate through a catheter until the reconnected bladder and urethra heal.

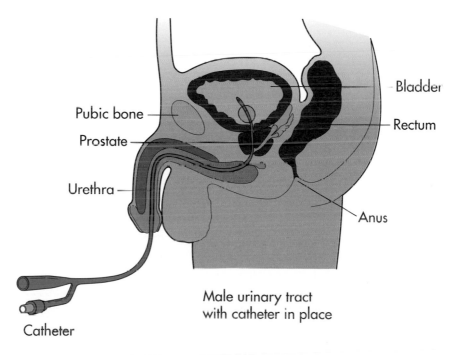

Pubic bone

Prostate

Urethra

Bladder

Rectum

Anus

Catheter

Male urinary tract
with catheter in place

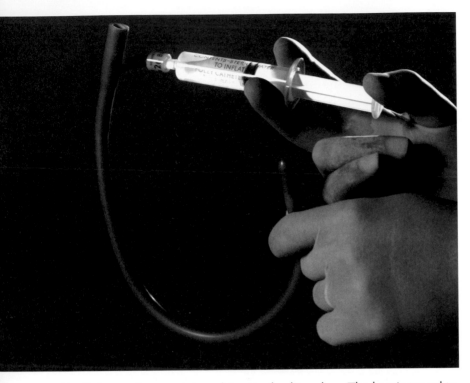

The Foley catheter, pictured, is attached to a bag. The bag is taped to the patient's leg and collects urine.

Still, using a catheter and urine bag can be discouraging. Patients say that keeping in mind that the situation is only temporary, helps them to maintain a sense of humor and make the best of an uncomfortable situation. John B. explains: "They took my prostate gland but left me with a new friend, who I called 'Foley' (the catheter). When you are tethered to someone in such an intimate way for 13 days, you get to be pretty tight. I was 100 percent continent [able to control urine flow] immediately after saying goodbye to Foley."[48]

Unlike John, many prostate cancer patients do not regain continence as soon as the catheter is removed. Problems with urine leakage after surgery may last up to a year. And, advanced prostate cancer can sometimes cause urinary problems, too. Wearing absorbent disposable incontinence products help. These include thick absorbent pads or diaper-like garments such as Depends. These items fit under a man's clothing and do not interfere with the wearer's mobility. Still, individuals must be careful to check the products often and change them when they are wet. "I measure out my days in diapers," Gottleib explains. "Do I need a change yet? Can I stretch the one I'm wearing another hour? Are the back of my pants okay?"[49]

Carrying around spare products helps individuals deal with the threat of leakage. William Martin recalls: "I discovered that one . . . pad slipped into a pair of jockey shorts gave me adequate protection . . . , though I usually carried a spare in the inside ticket pocket of my suit or blazer."[50]

Even so, the threat of leakage occurring in public can be quite stressful. It can cause some individuals to be uncomfortable in social situations and even avoid leaving home entirely. "A hermit is what I've become," Gottleib says.

> Even when she [his wife] can persuade me into going out, I'm not what you'd call an ideal guest. I smile and I chat, but my mind is always on my trouser's inseam, calculating rates of flow and absorption, the diuretic affects of alcohol and caffeine, and whether black jeans can truly hide a damp patch. When you're . . . far from the safety of home, you cannot let your mind wander lest you drop your defenses and wind up saying goodnight while side-stepping with your back against the wall as you head toward the front door.[51]

Fortunately, most urinary problems caused by surgery improve over time. First, patients stop leaking while reclining; then they regain control while walking. Finally, they are able to rise up from a sitting position without leaking. According to Korda, the bladder is, "like a bowl. When I was seated or lying down, it was turned on its side, so the urine tended to stay in it, but when I stood up the open end inverted, as if the bowl were turned upside down, and the urine simply ran out."[52]

How long it takes to reach the final stage depends on the individual. Doing special exercises, known as Kegel exercises,

Clinical Trials

When prostate cancer cannot be cured or contained with standard treatment, many individuals take part in a clinical trial. A clinical trial is a research study involving human subjects. Research institutes, drug companies, and hospitals sponsor clinical trials.

Some clinical trials test the effectiveness and safety of new medications. Others test combinations of medications, or new ways to administer medications.

All clinical trials are divided into three phases. Phase I aims to determine whether a particular treatment is safe for humans. Phase II focuses on establishing the treatment's effectiveness. Phase III compares the treatment's effectiveness to proven treatments.

Participation in a clinical trial is voluntary. All subjects receive some form of treatment without charge. In phase I and II, subjects are administered the test treatment. Because phase III compares the test treatment's effectiveness to proven treatments, in this phase some subjects receive the new treatment and some receive a proven treatment. Subjects are not aware of which form of treatment they receive.

helps speed up the process. Kegel exercises involve training the urinary sphincter muscles to contract so that a person can start and stop the flow of urine. Prostate cancer survivor and singer Harry Belafonte had problems with incontinence, "But because I was tenacious about doing the exercises, after one year it no longer existed,"[53] he explains.

Medications can also help urinary problems. And, for those individuals whose problems do not resolve naturally or with medication, surgery, in which an artificial sphincter is implanted around the urethra, provides a solution. So does sling surgery, a new type of surgery in which a strip of mesh is passed beneath the urethra. By supporting the part of the urethra most weakened by prostate cancer surgery, it helps prevent urine leakage.

Michael Yarborugh, a prostate cancer survivor with persistent urinary problems, underwent sling surgery. He explains: "It made a difference in my life, and I would recommend it to anyone suffering something similar."[54]

Coping with Erectile Dysfunction

Erectile dysfunction is another challenge many men with prostate cancer face. Surgery, radiation, and hormone therapy can all cause this problem. With time, many cases correct themselves. But for some men, the problem is permanent. Since many men feel that their ability to get and maintain an erection makes them masculine, erectile dysfunction not only presents a physical problem but also raises emotional issues. According to Belafonte, "The prostate is something that attacks that

Viagra is one option for men who may experience erectile dysfunction in the months following prostate surgery.

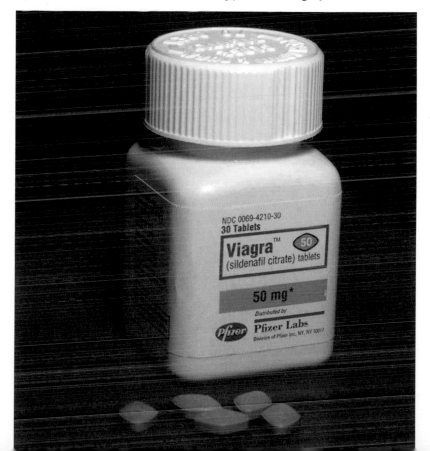

central part of the male body that men are very preoccupied with. Somehow, any disorder there means your life is over, you can't be a man anymore, you are now something less."[55]

Fortunately, there are a number of steps that prostate cancer patients can take to cope. Oral medications such as Viagra, for example, increase blood flow to the penis. Such drugs help many, but not all, men achieve an erection. Injecting a similar type of medication directly into the side of the penis minutes before sexual relations is another alternative. Because the needle that is used is small and thin, this procedure is painless. And, since the medication goes directly into the penis, it is more effective than oral medication. Prostate cancer survivor, Don, explains: "Penile injections work great . . . and they aren't as scary as they seem. It's a really tiny needle."[56]

Other men turn to a vacuum pump. This tube-like instrument is placed over the penis. When air is pumped into it, a vacuum is created sending blood into the penis. When the penis is erect, the pump is removed and a small rubber-band-like device is placed around the base of the organ. The band keeps the blood from flowing out of the penis and is removed after intercourse.

Finally, when other methods prove unsatisfactory, some prostate cancer patients have penile implant surgery. This involves the placement of silicon or inflatable rods into the penis. The silicon rods are semirigid at all times. The inflatable rods are connected to a pump, which is implanted in a man's scrotum, the sack that holds the testicles. Squeezing the pump fills the penis rods with salt water, facilitating intercourse. When intercourse is over squeezing a valve at the bottom of the pump returns the salt water to the pump, thereby deflating the rods.

Most prostate cancer patients say that with patience, and/or the help of one or more of these aids, they can and do overcome erectile problems. Ron puts it this way:

Most men are very concerned about their sex lives. I was certainly no exception there, and it was a major, major concern. There never seemed to be a fear that I was going to die, but it seemed like death that my sex life was over. Of course, I was exaggerating that in my own mind. There's nothing to be ashamed of. We are what we are, and we must take advantage of all the good things that we have. We still have our lives, and there is a sex life after prostate cancer.[57]

Managing Fatigue

Another challenge men with prostate cancer cope with is fatigue. The effects of surgery, radiation, and the disease itself all can cause fatigue. "One thing I really noticed after surgery," Torre recalls, "was a distinct energy loss. I felt that the fatigue came from a combination of factors which included the physical trauma of surgery, having the urinary catheter in for three weeks, and finally just the psychological fatigue that came from knowing I had cancer. Put them all together and you get pretty tired."[58]

Frequent urination, a common side effect of radiation therapy, adds to the challenge, causing individuals to get up repeatedly during the night in order to relieve themselves. According to Neider, "I must have been awakened nine or ten times to pee. After a while I had to concentrate hard to avoid getting angry. By morning I felt I was a wreck."[59]

Overwhelming fatigue makes it difficult for individuals to maintain their normal lives. Keeping a balance between activity and rest helps men with prostate cancer cope. Taking frequent naps, for example, allows individuals to conserve energy. Reducing regular activities also helps keep this balance. Such cutbacks often include reducing work hours or taking a leave of absence from work, curtailing social activities, and getting help with everyday tasks from friends, family members, or professional caregivers. For Torre, this meant taking an extended leave of absence from work. He explains:

The most difficult time came near the end of my recovery, when I was feeling pretty good during the day. But then I

Individuals undergoing treatment for prostate cancer will likely experience fatigue. If this occurs, it is important to rest and cut back on normal activity to conserve energy.

routinely found myself nodding off about 10 p.m. If I had been back managing the team, I would have been nodding off like that in the dugout in the sixth inning of a game. To do the job right, I needed to be able to stay awake until at least one or two o'clock in the morning, so I decided to hold off my return to the Yankees until I could do that.[60]

Dealing with Pain

Pain is another challenge. Although prostate cancer does not cause pain in its early stages, if the disease metastasizes individuals experience a high degree of pain. In addition, pain in the incision area after surgery is typical. And, because radiation therapy can damage near-by cells, it often causes pain in the rectum and pelvic area. Pain and burning in the anus during bowel movements due to swollen and inflamed rectal tissue is not uncommon with external radiation therapy. Neider describes his experience: "The anus burns fiercely both during the movement and for a couple of hours afterward. The pain is fatiguing. Resting in the lounger, afterwards, I feel my anus pulsing with pain."[61]

There are many ways men with prostate cancer deal with pain. Taking prescribed pain medication is one method. Exercise is another. It stimulates the production of endorphins, natural chemicals that give exercisers a feeling of well-being, thereby reducing feelings of pain. Exercise also combats fatigue, strengthens the body, and raises a person's spirits. Even if men with prostate cancer do not feel strong enough for vigorous exercise, low-impact exercises like walking or swimming help.

Korda started walking with his wife and a friend as soon as he returned home from the hospital:

From the very first morning, under a cold gray sky . . . the three of us, muffled to the gills against the cold, set off down the road outside our house, each of them holding on to an arm, as I shuffled breathlessly forward, trying

Low-impact exercises like walking or swimming can help an individual deal with the pain often associated with prostate cancer treatment.

to stand as upright as I could, holding my urine bag in a makeshift sling, determined to get to the end of our fenceline . . . I believe absolutely, without question, without doubt (and still believe) that the walk, lengthened every day, taken every morning even when the temperature plummeted . . . was what ultimately saved me from despair, fueled my recovery, brought me back at last from illness.[62]

Pursuing hobbies and other enjoyable activities, such as watching television, visiting with friends, reading, and listening to music may also help. Such activities focus the mind and distract an individual from painful sensations. Bert Gottleib found watching *Court TV* diverted his attention: "I was addicted to this judicial entertainment, the personalities of its players, and its fascinating quasi-scientific presentations. I was able to think about nothing else."[63]

In addition, men who are suffering from painful bowel movements and rectal burning find that making dietary changes often provides relief. Individuals say that avoiding spicy foods, which can make rectal burning worse, is one important change. Another is eating more creamy foods like dairy products, which makes bowel movements easier. "I avoid spicy foods to spare my inflamed insides and because such foods cause painful urination and bowel movements. I also indulge in heavy cream

Man to Man

Man to Man is the name of a special support program that helps men with prostate cancer throughout the United States. According to the American Cancer Society,

The Man to Man program helps men cope with prostate cancer by providing community-based education and support to patients and their family members . . . Man to Man plays an important role in community education about prostate cancer; it encourages men and health care professionals to actively consider screening for prostate cancer appropriate to each man's age and risk for the disease. A major part of the program is the self-help and/or support group. Volunteers organize free monthly meetings where speakers and participants learn about and discuss information about prostate cancer, treatment, side effects, and how to cope with the disease and its treatment.

In addition, Man to Man connects new prostate cancer patients with prostate cancer survivors, publishes a newsletter, and provides community outreach services to at risk groups such as African American men.

American Cancer Society, "Man to Man," www.cancer.org/docroot/ESN/content/ESN_3_1X_Man_to_Man_36.asp?sitearea=SHR.

to soothe the inner roasted areas, and lots of Jello,"[64] says Neider.

Coping with the Threat of Recurrence

Part of living with prostate cancer is coping with the threat of recurrence. With successful treatment, patients may remain cancer free for months or years. But there is always the possibility that prostate cancer will recur, either in the prostate, if it has not been surgically removed, or in other parts of the body where cancer cells that resisted the effects of treatment spread undetected. Doctors have no way of knowing whether this will happen. Patients with no evidence of cancer after treatment are said to be in remission. After five years without recurrence, patients are considered cured.

And, although the threat of a recurrence decreases over time and cure rates top 95 percent for men who undergo surgery or radiation, there are no guarantees. That is why prostate cancer patients go through frequent PSA monitoring. Testing is usually done once every three or four months for the first two years, once every six months for the next three years, and annually thereafter. A rise in PSA alerts patients and their physicians to the possibility of a recurrence. Not surprisingly, each doctor visit brings with it uncertainty and emotional stress. Actor and prostate cancer survivor Barry Bostwick explains: "My doctor feels my cancer was successfully treated with surgery. But when I'm forced to revisit the past by going for my bi-yearly PSA test, I once again feel vulnerability and sadness over the loss and diminishment of certain physical functioning and when I face the statistics, charts, and odds of recurrence, it still scares me."[65]

Even when PSA results are normal, knowing that the disease can recur at any time takes an emotional toll on prostate cancer survivors. Besides causing anxiety, it can make them feel that they are not in control of their lives. "Cancer engenders a particular kind of fear, because it is so insidious," says Berberich. "There is never a time when you can say you are free of it. Cancer follows you like a mental shadow that you have to beat back to remain in the light. Some can live with that better than others."[66]

Many men with prostate cancer make lifestyle changes in an effort to reduce the chance of recurrence. Losing weight, exercising, and making dietary changes help individuals feel more in control of their lives. Cutting back on dietary fats and red meat are common practices, as is taking nutritional supplements. In addition, many men consume more fruits, vegetables, and soy products since there is a possibility that these foods may offer protection against cancer. "I am not the same," says Korda. "I take vitamins, I bought and use a juicer. I eat more grains and fresh fruits and vegetables than ever."[67]

Dealing with Emotional Issues

The threat of recurrence, urinary incontinence, erectile dysfunction, pain, and fatigue all raise emotional issues. Men with prostate cancer report feeling angry, ashamed, stressed, frightened, and depressed. Indeed, because of changing hormone levels, depression is a common side effect of hormone

Participating in a support group is one way for men to cope with the physical and emotional challenges of prostate cancer.

therapy. Coping with these issues helps men to feel better and enjoy their lives more. One way some individuals do this is by talking to a mental health professional such as a counselor or psychologist.

Participating in a support group also helps men with prostate cancer face emotional challenges. It gives them an opportunity to discuss their feelings and anxieties and share their experiences with other cancer patients. Groups may consist only of prostate cancer patients, or be a mix of people with all kinds of cancer. Many hospitals sponsor support groups, as do community organizations and religious institutions. There are even Internet support groups for people who are unable to leave their homes.

"I think it's very valuable to belong to a support group," explains Henry, a prostate cancer survivor. "The more you talk about a problem you have, the easier it is to live with it. And you learn from other people. And if you talk about a subject, you're going to be more at ease, you're going to find out what's best to do and what's not."[68]

Clearly, men with prostate cancer face many challenges. Participating in a support group is just one of the many steps they take to cope. Taking such steps help individuals with prostate cancer to meet these challenges. In so doing, they improve the quality of their lives. Legendary golf pro and prostate cancer survivor Arnold Palmer puts it this way, "I would hope that we can overcome whatever ill effects [prostate cancer] might have on us, and get on with enjoying life."[69]

CHAPTER FIVE

What the Future Holds

Scientists are busily working on a variety of prostate cancer research projects. They are investigating ways to prevent the disease from occurring, developing new diagnostic methods, and creating new treatments.

Prevention

Researchers are looking at a number of different prevention strategies, many of which involve nutrition. Scientists already know that the body has natural defenses against cell mutation, but these defenses can be disturbed by environmental factors. For instance, cigarette smoke causes damage to cells in a person's lungs that leads to the development lung cancer. And, a high-fat diet is linked to prostate cancer. Therefore, scientists theorize that just as different environmental factors can negatively alter the body's defenses against cancer cell mutation, other environmental factors, like consuming certain nutrients, may help bolster the body's natural defenses and thus prevent or at least lower a man's risk of developing prostate cancer.

Among the nutrients being studied are isoflavones and polyphenols. Isoflavones are found in soy and polyphenols are found in green tea. Both of these foods are widely consumed in Asian countries, the part of the world with the lowest incidence of prostate cancer. Scientists hypothesize that low prostate cancer incidence and high intake of isoflavones and polyphenols may be linked. These nutrients, they theorize, may have a protective effect against prostate cancer.

Soy

Soy sources	Amount of soy protein
1 cup (8 ounces) soymilk	10 grams
4 ounces tofu	13 grams
1 soy burger	10–12 grams
1 soy protein bar	14–gram average
1 soy sausage link	6 grams
¼ cup roasted soy nuts	18–20 grams

Studies have shown that as little as two servings of soy a day has a positive effect on prostate health. This table highlights some common sources of soy.

It is already known that isoflavones are structurally similar to the female hormone estrogen, which, when it is administered to prostate cancer patients as a part of hormone therapy, inhibits testosterone production. Researchers think that when isoflavones are consumed in food, they act like a weak form of estrogen. Indeed, a number of studies have measured the effect of consuming soy on testosterone and PSA levels. One 2006 University of Hawaii, Honolulu, study put twelve healthy middle-aged men on a high soy diet and twelve on a low soy diet for one month, then the two groups switched diets. Men on the high soy diet were given two servings of soy a day, while the other group ate no soy. The men's testosterone and PSA levels were measured at the beginning and end of each month. Although neither group had any change in testosterone levels, both showed about a 14 percent decline in PSA after a month on the high soy diet. Based on these results, the researchers concluded that isoflavones in soy are not strong enough to inhibit testosterone production, but they do reduce the effect testosterone has on the prostate.

Other studies have yielded similar results both in healthy men and in men with prostate cancer. Says researcher Nadi B.

Kumar, who headed a 2004 Australian study that showed a 13 percent drop in PSA levels when subjects were fed 2 ounces (0.6kg) of soy per day for a month:

> Many previous studies have indicated that a soy-rich diet can prevent cancer development. But I am surprised at the results observed after only one month. That's pretty remarkable when you consider this disease has a long latency period—there's something like 16 to 20 years before you see evidence of prostate cancer. If men regularly consume this amount of soy over a lifetime, it has the promise of significantly reducing their risk of prostate cancer.[70]

Polyphenols found in green tea have also been the subject of a number of studies. In a 2003 study, researchers at the Burnham Institute, La Jolla, California, treated cancer cells in a laboratory with green teas, which caused the cells to destroy

A diet that includes soy and vegetarian foods is a good step in the prevention of prostate cancer.

Scientists are studying the positive effects of polyphenols on prostate cancer cells. Green tea, whether hot or iced, is a good source of polyphenols.

themselves. The scientists say that polyphenols contain a substance that prevents the production of a protein that keeps cancer cells from dying.

Ordinarily, defective cells destroy themselves. But cancer cells overproduce a protein, commonly known as the antideath protein, which keeps them from committing cell death. It appears that polyphenols stop the effectiveness of the antideath protein, thereby promoting cancer cell death. As a result of this study, scientists are currently testing polyphenols on animals and hope to begin human tests soon. If these tests yield similar results, green tea and green tea extracts could be used to both prevent and slow down the growth and spread of prostate cancer and possibly other forms of cancer.

In the meantime, it cannot hurt individuals to drink more green tea and eat more soy products. Says Joe Torre, "During the sixth inning of every game I have a soy shake and throughout the game I will drink anywhere from six to eight cups of iced green tea. Both are supposed to play a preventive role against prostate cancer and since I like the taste, it's not a problem."[71]

Fruits and Vegetables

Pomegranate juice is another food being investigated both as a prostate cancer preventative and as a way to reduce the chance of the disease recurring. It contains polyphenols and antioxidants. Antioxidants are substances that help protect cells against oxidation, a process in which cells are weakened when they come in contact with oxygen molecules. Weakened cells may be more likely to mutate. A 2006 University of California, Los Angeles, study looked at the effect of pomegranate juice on forty-eight men with recurrent prostate cancer who had been treated for prostate cancer through radiation therapy or surgery. At the start of the study, the men's PSA was tested. The men were treated with 8 ounces (.023kg) of pomegranate juice daily and their PSA levels were measured every three months. Before being treated with the juice, the men's PSA levels had been doubling about every fifteen months. By comparison, while drinking the juice the subject's PSA doubling time slowed to about fifty-four months. According to researcher Allan Pantuck, MD, "The velocity of the increase in PSA is decreased by 35 percent . . . We are hoping that pomegranate juice offers a novel strategy for prolonging doubling time in men who have been treated for prostate cancer. . . . For many men, this may extend the years after surgery or radiation that they remain recurrence free and their life expectancy is extended."[72]

Although more studies are being conducted on pomegranate juice, many healthcare providers are advising men to add the juice to their diet. Tomatoes and cruciferous vegetables (cabbage and turnips, for example) are other foods that also may help. Tomatoes contain powerful antioxidants called lycopenes. An ongoing Harvard University study known as the Health

Pomegranate juice is being investigated by scientists both as a prostate cancer preventative and as a way to reduce the chance of the disease recurring.

Professionals Follow-Up Study, has been looking at the effects of lifestyle and nutrition on the health of fifty thousand men since 1986. Every two years the men complete a questionnaire about their health, diet, and nutritional status, among other things. Although the study has not focused on prostate cancer, the researchers found that the subjects who consumed at least two servings of tomato sauce per week had a 28 percent decreased risk of developing prostate cancer confined to the prostate, and a 35 percent decreased risk of developing advanced prostate cancer than the subjects who did not eat these products. Interestingly, according to the study, cooked tomato products have a stronger effect on prostate cancer prevention than raw tomatoes. The reason for this is unclear. But it is possible that cooking changes the structure of lycopenes making them easier to absorb.

Other studies are focusing on cruciferous vegetables, such as cabbage, broccoli, cauliflower, kale, bok choy, and brussels sprouts. They contain sulforaphane, a substance that slows down cell mutation. In 2004, researchers at the University of Illinois, Urbana, theorized that eating a diet rich in sulforaphanes would slow down the cancer process and have a protective effect against prostate cancer. They further theorized that combining sulforaphanes with lypopenes would have an even more powerful effect. To prove their theory, the scientists fed mice with prostate cancer sulforaphane, alone, in the form of broccoli powder, lypopene, alone, in the form of tomato powder, and the two combined. All three treatments shrunk the tumors. With the tomato powder, tumors shrunk by 34 percent. Broccoli powder shrunk the tumors by 42 percent. When the two were combined, shrinkage rose to 52 percent. According to a report in the *Saturday Evening Post*, "The results suggest that

A diet rich in vegetables, especially tomatoes and cruciferous vegetables such as broccoli and cauliflower, is recommended not just for cancer prevention, but for overall health as well.

men concerned with prostate health may benefit by increasing both vegetables in their diets by consuming a comparable 1.4 cups of raw broccoli and 2.5 cups of fresh tomatoes (or 1 cup of tomato sauce daily), although the extent of the possible anti-cancer effects of these foods in humans is not yet known."[73]

Other tests on the effect of lypopenes and sulforaphanes have been inclusive or have produced conflicting results. So, scientists cannot say with certainty whether these substances do indeed protect the body against prostate cancer. Yet, since eating a diet rich in these nutrients has many other health benefits, healthcare professionals urge individuals to add them to their diet. "Regardless of whether studies have shown a benefit of particular fruits and vegetables in preventing the development or progression of prostate cancer, every person . . . should eat 5 to 9 servings a day of fruits and vegetables in accordance

Do Selenium and Vitamin E Help Prevent Prostate Cancer?

A number of studies indicate that vitamin E and selenium, a mineral found in plant foods, meat, and seafood, may help lower a man's risk of developing and/or dying of prostate cancer.

To help determine whether these nutrients can indeed help prevent prostate cancer, the National Institute of Health is sponsoring the Selenium and Vitamin E Chemoprevention Trial (SELECT). It is the largest cancer prevention trial examining the protective effects of nutritional supplements to ever be held. The trial, which began in 2001, involves thirty thousand men. One-third of the men are being given a selenium supplement, one-third are being given a vitamin E supplement, and one-third are being given a combination. The men's health will be monitored, and the effect of these supplements on the development of prostate cancer will be measured after seven and twelve years.

with the USDA's *Dietary Guidelines for America.*"[74] advises prostate cancer experts Peter H. Gann, MD, and Edward Giovannucci, MD.

Diagnosing and Prognosing

Other scientists are taking a different approach. They are trying to develop a diagnostic tool that will determine not only the presence of prostate cancer, but also whether the cancer is aggressive enough to require treatment. Currently a patient's Gleason score, cancer stage, and PSA levels are used to make a prognosis and determine treatment options. However, PSA can be deceiving. Both aggressive and slow growing prostate cancer raises PSA, as does aging, an enlarging prostate, and/or benign prostate conditions. And, although when PSA is extremely high, it correlates with aggressive prostate cancer, when Gleason scores are in the low to middle range and the cancer is in stage 1, it is difficult to know whether or not active treatment is sensible. As a result, some cases of slow growing prostate cancer are treated aggressively, which causes a host of side effects. In many cases, because the cancer is slow growing, such treatment is not necessary.

According to an article in *Time* magazine:

> Oncologists estimate that by age 50, as many as 4 out of 10 men have at least some cancerous cells in their prostate, cells that are likely to result in higher PSA readings. Yet of these men . . . only 8 % will eventually develop symptoms that affect their quality of life, and only 3 % will die of the cancer. . . . Says Dr. Otis Brawley, a senior investigator at the NCI, [National Cancer Institute] "treating some patients may end up doing more harm than good.". . . Much of the uncertainty could be eliminated, of course, if doctors could tell while a prostate cancer is still small, if it is lethally aggressive or a relatively benign type. In other words, whether a man will die of it or merely with it. The challenge . . . is to separate the pussycats from the tigers and identify aggressive tumors.[75]

To help meet this challenge, scientists are looking for a biomarker specific to aggressive prostate cancer. That is, a substance such as a protein or gene whose detection indicates the presence of a particular disease. If such a marker can be identified, it could help determine whether treatment is needed. Explains researcher Arul Chimaiyan, MD, of the University of Michigan, Ann Arbor:

> The molecular differences between metastatic prostate cancer and localized prostate cancer are not well established. . . . Our overall hypothesis is that metastatic (advanced) prostate cancer expresses genes that can be used to predict the aggressive potential of clinically localized prostate cancer. These "signature" lethal genes have potential as prognostic biomarkers, therapeutic targets, and may play a role in the progression from localized disease.[76]

To find such a marker, scientists are studying and comparing aggressive and nonaggressive prostate cancer cells that have been collected in prostate cancer tissue banks in locations throughout the United States. So far, a number of markers have been identified. One, found by researchers at the University of Michigan in 2002, is a gene called PAR-1. It is found in all prostate cancer cells, with the highest levels in those cells taken from subjects whose cancer has metastasized to the bones. Hence, identifying high levels of PAR-1 in biopsied prostate cancer cells could serve as a good indicator that the cancer is aggressive. However, because measuring PAR-1 is complex, at the current time this process is not feasible. But scientists are hoping to rectify this in the future.

Another marker known as B7-H3, which is easier to measure, was discovered in 2007 by researchers at the Mayo Clinic, Rochester, Minnesota. It is a protein found on the surface of normal, precancerous, and cancerous prostate cells. The level of B7-H3 directly correlates with the presence and aggressiveness of prostate cancer. According to the researchers, cells

with 19.8 percent or greater B7-H3 were four times more likely
to progress rapidly. In addition, even after treatment, cells with
higher levels of B7-H3 correlated with cancer recurrence, rais-
ing risk by 35 percent. Head researcher Eugene Kwon, MD,
explains: "Because B7-H3 is present in all prostate cancer
tumors, and marked levels predict recurrence, we are able to
forecast with much greater certainty the likelihood of cancer
progression."[77]

Because B7-H3 is such a recent discovery, pathologists are
not yet equipped to measure it. But scientists hope such meas-
urement will become part of prostate cancer biopsies in the
future. Evaluating B7-H3 levels will make it easier for healthcare professionals to determine which patients can safely opt
for expectant management and which need prompt treatment.
"This is the way of the future," Kwon explains.

> We are becoming educated about the ways to flesh out
> the molecular signature of each patient's cancer. Using
> such molecular signatures will facilitate for the first time,
> a truly individualized approach to prescribing the most
> appropriate therapy for a given patient. We will soon be
> able to tailor-make therapies for each person's cancer.[78]

Indeed, besides helping to determine the aggressiveness of
prostate cancer, B7-H3 may also become the target of prostate cancer treatment. In studying the protein, scientists have
learned that it protects cancer cells as they develop. Scientists
are unsure how B7-H3 does this, but they are conducting studies to try to find out. Once they can establish how B7-H3 oper-
ates, it may be possible to develop a form of treatment that
blocks B7-H3 from doing its job. And, because it appears that
B7-H3's only function in normal and precancerous prostate
cells is to facilitate prostate cancer's progression, scientists do
not think that targeting the protein would present a health risk.
However, until more is learned about B7-H3, development of
such a treatment remains a long-term goal.

Gene Therapy

Gene therapy is a new form of treatment that scientists are investigating. It involves replacing mutated oncogenes and tumor suppressor genes with healthy ones. Scientists theorize that the normal genes would signal the cancer cells to stop dividing, which would halt the cancer process.

Getting the genes into prostate cancer cells, however, is difficult. Genes cannot travel through the bloodstream on their own. They must be carried by something that can move easily through the bloodstream. And, once in the body, there is no guarantee that the carrier will reach the cancerous cells.

Scientists are solving this problem by modifying viruses. First, the virus' genes are removed. Then the viral genes are replaced with normal oncogenes and tumor suppressor genes. In the process, the virus is rendered harmless. Other modifications cause the virus to target prostate cells. When the modified virus is injected into the prostate, scientists think, it should deposit the healthy genes and halt the cancer process.

As of 2007, such therapy is still a long ways off, but it may be a possibility sometime in the future.

Targeted Treatments

Other new treatments should be available shortly. Many of these treatments are targeted treatments, therapies that aim to destroy cancer cells without harming healthy body cells or causing serious side effects. To accomplish this, targeted treatments use a variety of methods to attack cancer cells based on the specific way cancer cells differ from normal cells. One targeted treatment developed at Johns Hopkins University, Baltimore, Maryland, is already being tested in clinical trials. The treatment uses a genetically engineered protein, known as PRX302, which was created by modifying a protein made by prostate cancer cells. When PRX 302 comes in contact with prostate cancer cells, it attaches to the outside of the cells. The release of PSA by the cancer cells stimulates PRX302 to secrete a toxin that makes holes in the cancer cells, destroying them. The more PSA that is released, the more toxin PRX302 secretes.

Since more aggressive prostate cancer cells generally release higher quantities of PSA, the more aggressive the cancer, the more forceful the attack. Consequently, the treatment is customized to correlate with each individual's case. "This represents a different kind of target therapy, in that it seeks to use a protein made by the cancer to destroy itself,"[79] explains Johns Hopkins University's Sam Denmeade, who developed PRX302.

PRX302 is administered via injection directly into the prostate in much the same way as radioactive seeds are implanted. But because PRX302 affects only prostate cancer cells, it does not cause the side effects common to brachytherapy. Moreover, whereas up to one hundred radioactive seeds are generally implanted in brachytherapy, an amount of PRX302 about as large as one grain of salt can destroy a golf ball size tumor.

So far, scientists are optimistic about PRX302. The completion of one clinical trial in July 2007 at Scott and White Memorial Hospital, Temple, Texas, yielded encouraging results. In this trial, twenty-four men formerly treated with radiation therapy who showed signs of recurring prostate cancer confined to the prostate were treated with PRX302. The subjects' PSA was measured and they were administered a prostate biopsy before treatment began. PSA levels were then monitored thirty, sixty, and ninety days after treatment, and another biopsy was administered thirty days after treatment. The results were compared with the baseline tests. Thirty days after treatment, three of the subjects had no cancer cells at all in their biopsies, while fifteen others had a decrease in the percent of cancer cells.

Long-term PSA results were equally promising. These results were only gathered on fifteen subjects. Fourteen showed a decrease in PSA at least once during the PSA testing intervals. Moreover, after ninety days, eleven of the subjects showed a decrease in PSA. And, none of the patients exhibited any side effects from treatment. Researcher Scott Coffield explains: "The completion of the PRX302 . . . trial is encouraging from two perspectives. First there was therapeutic benefit demonstrated through overall PSA reduction in study patients, as well as a reduction in the number of positive biopsies after treatment. Second, there was no significant adverse side effect."[80]

More clinical trials must be conducted before PRX302 is approved as a safe and effective prostate cancer treatment. If the results of these trials are similar to those of the Scott and White trial, PRX302 could become a prostate cancer treatment option in just a few years.

What is even more encouraging is that PRX302 is just one of many new treatments being developed. It is clear that scientists are working hard in the fight against prostate cancer. The development of targeted treatments, new prevention strategies, and better diagnostic and prognostic tools offers hope to men with prostate cancer now and in the future.

Notes

Introduction: Lifesaving Information

1. Quoted in PBS, "Prostate Screening," February 13, 2003. www.pbs.org/newshour/bb/health/jan-june03/prostate_2-13.html.
2. Quoted in John Morgan, "Joe Torre Strikes Out Prostate Cancer," *USA Today*, June 10, 2003. www.usatoday.com/news/health/spotlighthealth/2003-06-10-torre_x.htm.
3. Quoted in The University of Texas M.D. Anderson Cancer Center, "Why Are Some Men Reluctant to be Screened for Prostate Cancer?" *CancerWise*, September 2000. www.cancerwise.org/September_2000/.
4. Quoted in The University of Texas M.D. Anderson Cancer Center, "Why Are Some Men Reluctant to be Screened for Prostate Cancer?"
5. Quoted in Clarence Waldron, "Minister Louis Farrakhan: Talks About Miraculous Recovery," *Jet Magazine*, March 5, 2007, p. 5.
6. Bert Gottlieb and Thomas Mawn, *The Men's Club*. Oxnard, CA: Pathfinder, 1999, p. 40.

Chapter 1: What is Prostate Cancer?

7. Patrick Walsh and Janet Farrar Worthington, *Dr. Patrick Walsh's Guide to Surviving Prostate Cancer*. New York: Warner Books, 2002, p. 45.
8. Robert A. Weinberg, "How Cancer Arises," *Scientific American*, September 1996, p. 62.
9. Robert A. Weinberg, *One Renegade Cell*. New York: Basic Books, 1998, p. 1.
10. F. Ralph Berberich, *Hit Below the Belt*. Berkeley, CA: Celestial Arts, 2001. p. 47.
11. David Nawrocki, "Living in the Nanosecond: My Prostate Cancer Clock," *PSA Rising*, December 7, 1998. http://psa-rising.com/voices/david_nawrocki.htm.

12. Quoted in John Cummins, "The Importance of Prostate Exams," *American Profile.com*, November 26, 2006. www.americanprofile/com/article/19915.html.
13. Quoted in David G. Botswick, E. David Crawford, Celestia S. Higano, and Mack Roach III, eds., *American Cancer Society's Complete Guide to Prostate Cancer*. Atlanta: American Cancer Society, 2005, p. 17.
14. Quoted in Nicole Fawcett, "A Bond of Brothers: Siblings and Prostate Cancer," *PSA Rising*, September 22, 2004. www.psa-rising.com/med/gene/brothers_pca.html.
15. Quoted in Nicole Fawcett, "African-Americans with Prostate Cancer More Likely to Have a Family History of Prostate, Breast Cancer: U-M Study," University of Michigan Comprehensive Cancer Center, November 29, 2006. www.cancer.med.umich.edu/news/family_history06.shtml.
16. Quoted in Botswick, Crawford, Higano, and Roach, eds., *American Cancer Society's Complete Guide to Prostate Cancer*, p. 8.
17. Quoted in PSA Rising, "African American Prostate Cancer Crisis," December 26, 1998. http://psa-rising.com/medicalpike/africanamer.htm.
18. Quoted in Jacqueline Strax, "Racial Difference Found in Androgen Receptor in Men with Prostate Cancer." *PSA Rising*, September 4, 2003. www.psa-rising.com/med/african-am/raceAR92003.shtml.
19. Quoted in American Cancer Society, "Lose Weight, Reduce Prostate Cancer Risk?" December 22, 2006. http://www.cancer.org/docroot/NWS/content/NWS_1_1x_Lose_Weight_Reduce_Prostate_Cancer_Risk.asp
20. Michael Korda, *Man to Man*. New York: Vintage Books, 1997. p. 7.

Chapter 2: Diagnosing Prostate Cancer

21. Korda, *Man to Man*. p. 12.
22. William Martin, *My Prostate and Me*. New York: Cadell & Davies, 1994. p. 58.
23. Korda, *Man to Man*. p. 12.
24. Charles Neider, *Adam's Burden*. Lanham, MD: Madison Books, 2001. p. 4.

25. Andy Grove, "Taking on Prostate Cancer," *Fortune Magazine*, May 13, 1996. www.usrf.org/news/010815-Andy_Grove_CaP.html.
26. Quoted in Botswick, Crawford, Higano, and Roach, eds., *American Cancer Society's Complete Guide to Prostate Cancer*, p. 50.
27. Berberich, *Hit Below the Belt*, p.18.
28. Gottleib and Mawn, *The Men's Club*, p. 12.
29. Quoted in PBS, "Prostate Screening."
30. Gottleib and Mawn, *The Men's Club*, p. 24.
31. Gottleib and Mawn, *The Men's Club*, p. 29.
32. Quoted in Botswick, Crawford, Higano, and Roach, eds., *American Cancer Society's Complete Guide to Prostate Cancer*, p.150.

Chapter 3: Treating Prostate Cancer

33. Berberich, *Hit Below the Belt*, p.35
34. Quoted in Mayo Clinic, "Prostate Cancer Guide, Meet Thomas Sellers," February 15, 2007. http://mayoclinic.com/health/prostate-cancer/PC99999/Page=PC00031.
35. Quoted in Botswick, Crawford, Higano, and Roach, eds., *American Cancer Society's Complete Guide to Prostate Cancer*, p. 163.
36. Paul H. Lange and Christine Adamec, *Prostate Cancer for Dummies*. New York: Wiley, 2003, p. 124
37. Quoted in Urological Science Research Foundation (USRF), "New York Yankees Manager, Joe Torre," *Johns Hopkins Prostate Bulletin*. www.usrf.org/news/010815-Joe_Torre_CaP.html.
38. Quoted in Prostate-Help (blog), "The Stories," July 21, 2005. http://prostate-help.blogs.com/stories/2005/07/pete_diagnosed_.html#more.
39. Quoted in Mayo Clinic, "Prostate Cancer Guide, Meet Thomas Sellers."
40. Judy Eberhardt, "Curing Mr. Right," *Good Housekeeping*, September 2005, p. 98.
41. Berberich, *Hit Below the Belt*, p. 159.
42. Quoted in Mayo Clinic, "Prostate Cancer Guide, Meet Paul Patrick," February 15, 2007. http://mayoclinic.com/health/

prostate-cancer/PC99999/Page=PC00030&.

43. Quoted in Mayo Clinic, "Prostate Cancer Guide, Meet Charles Jennings," February 15, 2007. http://mayoclinic. com/health/prostate-cancer/PC99999/Page=PC00029.

44. Quoted in David Kirby, "More Options, and Decisions, for Men With Prostate Cancer," *New York Times*, October 3, 2000. http://www.phoenix5.org/articles/NYtimes100300. html

45. Korda, *Man to Man*, p. 239.

Chapter 4: Living with Prostate Cancer

46. Quoted in Sharon Brown, "Goulet Dreams of Cancer Cure," *South Bend Tribune*, May 24, 1996. www.usrf.org/ news/Robert_Goulet.html.

47. Korda, *Man to Man*, p. 156

48. Quoted in Botswick, Crawford, Higano, and Roach, eds., *American Cancer Society's Complete Guide to Prostate Cancer*, p. 177.

49. Gottleib and Mawn, *The Men's Club*, p. 141.

50. Martin, *My Prostate and Me*, p. 203.

51. Gottleib and Mawn, *The Men's Club*, pp.141–42.

52. Korda, *Man to Man*, p. 196.

53. Quoted in Phoenix5, "Why Harry Belafonte Talks About Prostate Cancer," *Los Angeles Times*, April 21, 1997. www.phoenix5.org/stories/famous/Belafonte.html.

54. Quoted in Medical News Today, "Help for Prostate Cancer Survivors Who Suffer from Urinary Incontinence," September 1, 2007. www.medicalnewstoday.com/ articles/80936.php.

55. Quoted in Phoenix5, "Why Harry Belafonte Talks About Prostate Cancer."

56. Quoted in Botswick, Crawford, Higano, and Roach, eds., *American Cancer Society's Complete Guide to Prostate Cancer*, p. 305.

57. Quoted in Botswick, Crawford, Higano, and Roach, eds., *American Cancer Society's Complete Guide to Prostate Cancer*. p. 302.

58. Quoted in USRF, "New York Yankees Manager, Joe Torre."

59. Neider, *Adam's Burden*, p. 107.
60. Quoted in USRF, "New York Yankees Manager, Joe Torre."
61. Neider, *Adam's Burden*, p.123.
62. Korda, *Man to Man*, p. 183.
63. Gottleib and Mawn, *The Men's Club*, p. 143.
64. Neider, *Adam's Burden*, p. 139.
65. Quoted in Botswick, Crawford, Higano, and Roach, eds., *American Cancer Society's Complete Guide to Prostate Cancer*, p. 317.
66. Berberich, *Hit Below the Belt*, p. 46.
67. Korda, *Man to Man*, p. 206.
68. Quoted in Neider, *Adam's Burden*, p. 229.
69. Quoted in Barbara Payne, "The Legend Continues . . . After Prostate Cancer," usrf.org. http://www.usrf.org/news/010815-Arnold_Palmer_CaP.html.

Chapter 5: What the Future Holds

70. Quoted in Sid Kirchheimer, "Soy Improves Prostate Cancer Outlook," WebMD, September 24, 2004. www.webmd.com/prostate-cancer/news/20040924/soy-improves-prostate-cancer-outlook.
71. Quoted in USRF, "New York Yankees Manager, Joe Torre."
72. Quoted in PSA Rising, "Pomegranate Juice Slows PSA Rise in Men with Recurrent Prostate Cancer." http://www.psa-rising.com/eatingwell/pomegranate-juice06.htm
73. *Saturday Evening Post*, "Broccoli Plus Tomatoes Fight Prostate Cancer," May–June 2007, p. 62.
74. Peter H. Gann and Edward L. Giovannucci, *Nutrition and Prostate Cancer*. Santa Monica, CA: Prostate Cancer Foundation, 2005, p. 12.
75. Quoted in Leon Jaroff, "The Man's Cancer," *Time*, April 1, 1996. www.usrf.org/news/010815-Norman_Schwarzkopf_CaP.html.
76. Quoted in Evan Keller, "Research Projects," University of Michigan Comprehensive Cancer Center. www.cancer.med.umich.edu/research/spore research projects.shtml.

77. Quoted in Mayo Clinic, "First Biomarker Discovered that Predicts Prostate Cancer Outcome," August 15, 2007. www.mayoclinic.org/news2007-rst/4188.html.
78. Quoted in Mayo Clinic, "First Biomarker Discovered that Predicts Prostate Cancer Outcome."
79. Quoted in Medical News Today, "Scientists Design a PSA Activated Protoxin that Kills Prostate Cancer," November 14, 2006. www.medicalnewstoday.com/articles/56374.php
80. Quoted in Protox, "Protox Announces Positive Clinical Data From Prostate Cancer Study," July 10, 2007. www. protoxtherapeutics.com/news/2007/0328015.php.

Glossary

androgen: Name given to male sex hormones.

antioxidants: Substances that help protect cells against oxidation, a process in which cells are weakened when they come in contact with oxygen molecules.

benign prostatic hyperplasia (BPH): A condition caused by hormonal changes as a man ages, which accelerates prostate growth.

benign tumor: A relatively harmless mass composed of normal cells.

biopsy: A sample of tissue taken from a tumor for medical analysis.

bladder: The organ that stores urine.

brachytherapy: A form of radiation therapy in which radioactive seeds are implanted in the prostate.

cancer: A condition caused by the uncontrolled and purposeless growth of cells, which can spread throughout the body.

catheter: A flexible tube that is inserted into the body to drain fluid.

digital rectal exam (DRE): An examination of the prostate in which a gloved lubricated finger is inserted into the rectum.

erectile dysfunction (impotence): The inability to get or maintain an erection.

expectant management (watchful waiting): Closely monitoring prostate cancer without administering treatment.

gene: The part of a cell that provides inherited information.

Gleason grading system: System used to rate the aggressiveness of prostate cancer cells.

grade: A way to classify the aggressiveness of cancer cells.

hormone therapy: A prostate cancer treatment that uses hormones to halt the production of testosterone.

incontinence: The unintentional passing of urine.

isoflavones: Substance found in soy products that may have a preventive effect against prostate cancer.

Kegel exercises: Exercises that train the urinary sphincter muscles to contract so that a person can start and stop the flow of urine.

laprascopic radical prostectomy (LPR): Removal of the prostate gland using a telescoping camera and tiny instruments that are inserted through small incisions.

lycopenes: Substance found in tomatoes that may have a preventive effect against prostate cancer.

malignant tumor: A mass composed of cancer cells.

metastasis: The spread of cancer throughout the body.

oncogene: Gene that signals cells to divide.

oncologist: A doctor who specializes in the treatment of cancer.

pathologist: A doctor who studies and analyzes body tissue in a laboratory.

polyphenols: Substance found in green tea and some fruits that may have a preventive effect against prostate cancer.

prognosis: An estimate of how likely the patient is to be cured, or what his long-term survival chances are.

prostate gland: A small walnut-shaped gland that is part of the male reproductive system.

prostate specific antigen (PSA): A protein produced by

the prostate. High levels in the blood can indicate prostate cancer.

prostatectomy: The surgical removal of all or part of the prostate gland.

prostatitis: An inflammation of the prostate usually caused by a bacterial infection.

PSA velocity: The rate PSA levels increase over time.

radiation therapy: The use of high energy rays to destroy cancer cells.

remission: A disappearance of all signs of cancer as a result of treatment.

seminal vesicules: Male reproductive organs attached to the prostate, which help in the production of seminal fluid.

stage: A way to classify how far cancer has spread.

testosterone: Male hormone that is needed for prostate growth and the production of seminal fluid.

transrectal ultrasound (TRUS): An imaging procedure that uses sound waves to produce images of the prostate gland.

tumor suppressor gene: Gene that signals cells to stop dividing.

urethra: Tube that carries seminal fluid and urine out of the body.

urologist: A physician who specializes in conditions that involve the kidney, bladder, prostate gland, penis, and testicles.

Organizations to Contact

American Cancer Society

1599 Clifton Rd. NE
Atlanta, GA 30329
(800) 227-2345
www.cancer.org

The American Cancer Society is a national organization with local groups throughout the country. It offers information on all types of cancer and sponsors support groups such as Man to Man.

National Prostate Cancer Coalition

1154 15th Street, NW
Washington, DC 20005
(888) 245-9455
www.fightprostatecancer.org/site/PageServer

Offers information about prostate cancer prevention and treatment as well as links to articles about recent research results.

Prostate Cancer Foundation

1250 4th Street, Suite 360
Santa Monica, CA 90401
(800) 757-2873
www.prostatecancerfoundation.org

A good source of information, survivor stories, nutritional research, and free publications on prostate cancer.

Prostate Cancer Research Institute
5777 W. Century Blvd, Suite 800
Los Angeles, CA 90045
(800) 641-PCRI
www.prostate-cancer.org/index.html

This organization's objective is to educate people about prostate cancer. Offers information about every aspect of prostate cancer, a newsletter, and sponsors an annual conference.

US Too, International
5003 Fairview Ave.
Downers Grove, IL 60515
(630) 795-1002
Support Hotline (800-808-7866)
www.ustoo.com/

A prostate cancer education and support network providing information on all aspects of prostate cancer, a support hotline, and contact information for support groups throughout the world.

For More Information

Books

Scott D. Cramer, *Prostate Cancer*. Philadelphia: Chelsea House, 2007. An informative book for young adults.

Peter H. Lange, MD, and Christine Adamec, *Prostate Cancer for Dummies*. Indianapolis: Wiley, 2003. A simple and clear adult book about prostate cancer with amusing cartoons and helpful icons.

Mark Stokes, MD, *Prostate Cancer: Current and Emerging Trends in Detection and Treatment*. New York: Rosen, 2006. A young adult book focusing on prostate cancer screening, treatment, and new technologies.

Lisa Yount, *Cancer*. San Diego: Lucent Books, 1999. An informative young-adult book that looks at cancer in general.

Periodicals

Judy Eberhardt, "Curing Mr. Right," *Good Housekeeping*, September 2005.

John Morgan, "Joe Torre Strikes Out Prostate Cancer," *USA Today*, June 10, 2003.

Robert A. Weinberg, "How Cancer Arises," *Scientific American*, September 1996.

Internet Sources

MSNBC, "Prostate Cancer News and Information," www.msnbc.msn.com/id/13154507/

PBS.org, "Prostate Screening," www.pbs.org/newshour/bb/health/jan-june03/prostate_2-13.html

Web Sites

James Buchanan Brady Urological Institute (http://urology.jhu.edu/index.html) A part of Johns Hopkins hospital, the web site has articles and videos about different prostate cancer treatments.

Mayo Clinic.com (http://mayoclinic.com/health/prostate-cancer/PT99999) A variety of information about prostate cancer including articles about prostate cancer survivors and their treatment.

Phoenix5 (www.phoenix5.org/menumain.html) Dedicated to helping men with prostate cancer and their families; provides information, survivor stories, and links.

The University of Texas M.D. Anderson Cancer Center (www.mdanderson.org/diseases/prostate/) A good source of prostate cancer information including survivor stories, a message board, and links to support groups.

USRF (www.usrf.org/index.shtml) The web site of the Urological Sciences Research Foundation provides a wealth of information including articles and interviews with celebrity prostate cancer survivors, current research news, and information on nutrition and prostate cancer.

Index

Picture Credits

Cover photo: © 2008/Jupiterimages
AJPhoto/Photo Researchers, 43
AP Images, 9, 26, 50, 61
Colin Cuthbert/Photo Researchers, 47
© 2008 Custom Medical Stock Photo. All rights reserved,
        11, 58
Jim Dowdalls/Photo Researchers, 19
Field Mark Publications, 73
Gale, Cengage Learning, 14, 17, 31, 45, 57, 72
© iStockphoto.com, 24
© iStockphoto.com/Gary Sludden, 29
© iStockphoto.com/Graca Victoria, 76
© iStockphoto.com/Marcel Mooij, 66
© iStockphoto.com/Satu Knape, 74
© iStockphoto.com/Steve Luker, 64
© iStockphoto.com/Ulrich Willmunder, 77
Will and Deni McIntyre/Photo Researchers, 69
Phanie/Photo Researchers, 36
SPL/Photo Researchers, 15
© 2008 David Weinstein & Associates/Custom Medical
        Stock Photo. All rights reserved, 33

About the Author

Barbara Sheen is the author of more than forty nonfiction books for young people. She lives in New Mexico with her family. In her spare time she likes to swim, walk, cook, read, and garden.